ISADORA'S CHRISTMAS PLIGHT

A CHRISTMAS STORY

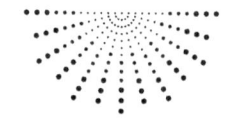

ROSIE SWAN

Publisher's Note: This is a work of fiction. Names, characters, places, and incidents are a product of the author's imagination. Locales and public names are sometimes used for atmospheric purposes. Any resemblance to actual people, living or dead, or to businesses, companies, events, institutions, or locales is completely coincidental.

© 2021 PUREREAD LTD

PUREREAD.COM

CONTENTS

1. Out of the Shadows — 1
2. Dreamer in the Valley — 17
3. The Bond Husband — 23
4. Dark Night — 27
5. Just an Illusion — 39
6. Maiden's Penance — 49
7. The Forgotten Path — 57
8. The Dark Rainbow — 64
9. Unfolding Destiny — 70
10. Hour of Light — 74
11. Healing Waters — 80
12. The Bridge Builder — 84
13. The Open Door — 89
14. Weep No More — 94
15. A Matter of Time — 99
16. Up in Flames — 102
17. Abyss of Thought — 105
18. Edge of the Sword — 108
19. Nothing in the Dreams — 114
20. The Healing Petals of Christmas — 117
21. Troubled Thoughts — 123
22. Hidden Danger — 126
23. The Broken Rose — 129
24. The Stripped Twilight — 131
25. Hour of Darkness — 145
26. Wave of Secrets — 148
27. The Maiden's Tears — 154
28. Silken Truth — 162
29. Valley of Decision — 165

Our Gift To You — 173

1

OUT OF THE SHADOWS

CHRISTMAS DAY - DOWNTOWN LONDON - 1840

On the morning of December the twenty fifth, better known as Christmas Day, exactly forty years into the nineteenth century, a little baby girl was born. The clear evidence of her birth was the screaming and cursing of the woman who brought her forth into the world, and the chuckling of the midwife with blackened teeth due to the chewing of too much tobacco. To Rita Bower, the young mother, it was an agonizing twelve hours and she was glad when the baby finally came out of her and into the world. The little girl announced her arrival into the world with a lusty cry, causing the midwife to shake her head, a huge smile on her tired face. The task of delivering this baby had been hard on both mother and midwife and she was glad it was all over now.

These London socialites refused to get married to good men back in the countryside where most came from. Instead, they came to London and allowed themselves to become mistresses to wealthy men, who provided for their every need. In order to further ensnare the poor men who were so besotted with them, from time to time, they would bear children and use them as a means to continue enjoying the kind of life they were accustomed to. Still, they paid good money for her services and she wasn't complaining. At least this little one had come out alive and the young woman hadn't given her instructions to ensure that it stopped breathing as soon as it was born. Many did and also entrusted her with the task of getting rid of the small lifeless bodies. That, of course, made her fees much higher but lately she was finding it very difficult to dispose of the corpses. London was changing and now there were policemen at every corner of the street taking note of any suspicious movements. Twice, she'd nearly been caught carrying dead babies and only her wit and shrewdness had saved her. But she was getting too old for this kind of life.

"This one sure has got a powerful set of lungs on her," the midwife said as she held out the wailing baby to her mother.

"Put her in the crib," the angry woman said, waving her away. She refused to even look at the child. "Get her away from me."

"I see no crib in this room, Miss Bower."

"Put her on the floor or anywhere you deem fit," Rita struggled to get out of bed. "Now, I have to prepare myself for my guest."

"You only just brought forth a baby, don't you think it's too soon for that?" The midwife placed the child on a floor in one corner as she cleaned up the room. All the furniture in this front room had been pushed to one side to make room for the delivery to take place with as little mess as possible. The midwife started putting things back in the order she'd found them. As she did so, she thought about this young woman who was one of her many customers. This one had it better than most, what with a man who had set her up in her own three-bedroom two story house. It was also well furnished and she dressed well, but like most London socialites, even that wasn't enough for her.

"The rent is due and there's no food in this house. How do you expect me to survive and also pay your fees?"

"Miss Bower, it's not safe for you to do that, especially not now. You won't last long in the world at this rate."

Rita snorted, barely glancing at her baby whose cries had faded into soft whimpers. "Who cares about lasting long in this world? All I need is something to eat and pay the rent so I won't be turned out into the streets."

"What about your baby? Who will take care of her when you're occupied with your various pursuits?" The midwife looked around. "This house was set up for you by a wealthy man, why doesn't he pay the rent for you?"

Rita shrugged and turned away, making the midwife know that she had done something to her benefactor and that was why he'd stopped taking care of her.

"At least consider the little one and nurse her. She'll sleep and you can then do whatever you want."

"The sooner she learns to take care of herself, the better for everyone. Now, I only have a few coins but if you come back in the evening, I'll have all your money for you."

The midwife shook her head as she finished rearranging the room and then surveyed her work.

"You need to be careful because of your condition, Miss Bower. This child survived while you managed to rid yourself of the previous ones. One more pregnancy could kill you."

"I'll be careful," she glanced briefly at the child in the corner. "I tried to get rid of this one but she was too stubborn. No matter how many times I attempted, she just wouldn't come out. Now she has to learn to take care of herself."

There was a knock at the front door and the two women looked at each other. "Who do you think it is?" Rita asked fearfully, moving away from the door.

The midwife shrugged, "I don't live here you do, so you should know who your visitors are."

The knock was firm and persistent and Rita finally opened the door. Edgar Fontaine stood in the doorway and surveyed the room.

"What's going on here?" he looked around then heard a sound like that of a little cat. "Did you get a cat?"

"This one just had a baby," the midwife blurted out and ignored the glare from her patient. "She's still very weak but won't stay in bed because there's nothing in the house for her to eat. Her paps are dry and the little one needs milk and her rent's also due, poor lamb."

Edgar looked at the beautiful woman standing in front of him. "Rita, is that my baby?" He asked in a soft voice. She nodded but kept her head down. "Why didn't you tell me that you were pregnant by me? Was that why you avoided me?" He held her gently by the shoulders, "Did you think I would abandon you and our child?"

"Edgar," she said in her most seductive voice, "You're a married man and I didn't want to cause you any trouble," she said. "This is my problem."

"Rita, please don't say that. You know that I care about you and that's why I got you this house, so you could live in a comfortable place." He turned toward the corner where the child was. "Is it a boy?"

"No, it's a girl," the midwife was watching the exchange with much interest. The gentleman who'd just come into the room looked like a person of means and if she played her cards right, she could walk out of here with more than just her maternity fees. So, he was the one who had set this socialite up. "She is really beautiful but hungry."

"Here, sit down," Edgar took Rita's hand and led her to the large couch. "Why is the child on the floor?" He turned to the midwife. "Couldn't you place her on the couch or anywhere else? The floor must be cold and that's probably why she's crying so much."

"We didn't want to mess up any of the furniture during the delivery and I was just cleaning up when you came in," the woman responded. "I would have eventually gotten her to the couch," and saying so, she walked over to the corner and picked the baby up. "Hush little one," she crooned.

"What's your name, Ma'am?"

"They call me Stella Lugard," she said.

"Mrs. Lugard, may I impose on your time please?"

"Whatever you need, sir."

"I was coming to visit Rita but had no idea that this was going on," Edgar said. "Now that there's a baby, I need to purchase this house for her so she will never have to worry about the rent again. This is a good place and I promise," he touched Rita's cheek, "That I'll take good care of you and my child. But Rita will need a lot of help since she now has my baby to take care of."

"Whatever you need, sir," Stella had a sly look in her eyes but Edgar didn't care, his mistress and daughter would be taken care of, that's all that mattered to him.

Eight Years Later

Isadora couldn't understand what was going on outside there. She could hear murmurs coming from her mother's bedroom but she was in the closet right next to the landing where she'd always been told to hide whenever visitors came to the house. There wasn't the usual laughter and it sounded like her mother was crying but she couldn't be sure. Her knees were tired from kneeling in the small dark closet and she also desperately needed to answer the call of nature. Something fell, startling her and she started crying but softly so she wouldn't get into trouble. She wanted her mother but if she dared leave the closet, her ears would be boxed.

The door opened and then was slammed and heavy footsteps walked down the small corridor and past the closet, down the stairs and then she heard the front door open and that was also slammed. That could only mean that the visitor had gone and she opened the closet door and peeked out, too scared to come out at first.

The gas lamp cast eerie shadows on the walls and she suddenly felt afraid. Usually after her mother's visitor would leave, Rita would emerge from the bedroom, a silly smile on her face. She would then call out to Isadora and together they would walk down the stairs to the kitchen to prepare dinner. The next day, they would go shopping for her mother would have money to spend on her many indulgences and Isadora would also get a pretty trinket as her reward for staying out of the way.

But Isadora waited for her mother to come out from her bedroom but a long time passed and that didn't happen. Feeling the pressure to relieve herself, the child burst out of the closet and ran to the small privy down the stairs. Once she was done, she climbed back up the stairs to find her mother.

"Mama?" She called out in a fearful voice, tiptoeing to the bedroom whose door had been slammed shut by the visitor who'd just left. "Mama?" Her hand reached for the knob and she felt very weak but forced herself to turn it and push it open.

Then she saw her mother lying on the floor and there was a pool of blood around her. That was when Isadora screamed with all her might.

"Where are we going?" Isadora turned her green eyes to the man she knew to be her father. "Papa?"

"I'm taking you home to the country side to live with me," he said then turned back to his newspaper. He hadn't spoken much to her since he had arrived at the house early that morning. She had no idea who had informed him about her mother's death two days ago but he'd come and after the burial, had told her to pack whatever she felt was important because he was taking her away.

From time to time, he would pat her on the head but his concentration was on the paper he was reading. It was left to her to keep herself entertained and she turned her face toward the window so he wouldn't see her crying.

She missed her mother so much but the priest had explained to her that her mother had gone to be in a better place. Isadora had longed to ask the priest why her mother hadn't taken her away if wherever she had gone was better than where they were, but the words just wouldn't come out. All she knew was that she would never see her mother again and it made her sad and frightened.

The events of the past two days flashed through her mind and she moaned softly, clutching at her stomach as if in pain. After discovering her mother's body, she had screamed while pleading for her to open her eyes. The neighbours had broken down the front door and then called the constable. From then on it had been hours of questioning as the constable tried to ascertain who had killed her mother. Did she see who had come into the house? And always her answer had been just to shake her head. Whenever her mother had been expecting her visitors, she would tell Isadora to hide in the closet before they arrived, so she never once saw any of them.

The only man she was allowed to meet was her father and he made the journey from Oxford to London once a month. He never stayed more than a few hours at most and she loved it when he visited for he would bring her new dresses and shoes, and then there would be delicacies for her to eat.

"Don't ever tell your father about my friends," her mother had told her years ago. *"He won't understand."*

"Why Mama?"

"Because I am a beautiful woman and have many friends," her mother had said, flicking her thick dark hair over her shoulders. Isadora got her green eyes and dark hair from her mother. *"If you want to continue getting*

new dresses and good things, don't ever tell your father about my friends."

And Isadora had been sworn to secrecy. Now as the carriage swayed, taking her away from the only place she'd known for the first eight years of her life, she wished that she had peeked to see who it was that had murdered her mother.

~

Edgar Fontaine pretended to read the newspaper so he didn't have to answer the child's questions. She was a very beautiful and obedient child and he knew that he couldn't leave her in London, not after her mother's death.

The constable had been vague in his explanations but Edgar knew that Rita had been murdered by one of her many lovers. Years ago, when he first met her, she'd been a chorus girl at the London Theatre. Her beauty had dazzled him and he found himself attending all her sessions that month. At the end of it when he heard that her troupe would be leaving for Bristol for six months, he'd approached her and begged her to stay in London.

"I love you," he'd told her, so taken in by her beauty that he'd even forgotten that he had a wife and son back in Oxford. He just had to have her and that had led to a year of unforgettable passion, at least on his side. But Rita got bored and began demanding that he should leave his wife for her. He had very nearly done so but then found out that he wasn't the only man in her life.

When he'd confronted her, she'd sobbed and told him that she was so lonely when he was away and also afraid of being alone where she lived. So he'd rented her a better house and when Isadora was born, he'd bought the property for her. That was the same house she'd been murdered in and then he found out that she'd tried to sell the house on more than one occasion. Good thing was that the deed was in his name and that's how the house had been saved. Before returning to Oxford, he'd made arrangements for the house to be sold and the money placed in a trust for Isadora. When she turned twenty-one, she would have access to the funds and do whatever she wanted with it.

The moment Edgar had looked into Isadora's sweet green eyes on the day she was born, he knew that she wasn't really his child but he couldn't leave her. There was something about the baby that drew him and he accepted the lies Rita told him. The only thing that happened was that this time, he put his foot down and told her that she had to stop selling her favours since he would take care of the two of them. He should have known that a woman like Rita couldn't stay faithful or keep any promises and that's what had led to the end of their relationship when Isadora was one year old. But he hadn't stopped taking care of them, for the child's sake and because he felt a strong obligation toward her.

But apparently he'd only made it easier for her to keep her numerous lovers and finally, one of them had ended her life. He didn't know what his wife was going to say when he brought Isadora to the house. Of course, Clarissa knew about his indiscretions years ago before he changed and decided that having a wife and a mistress at the same time wasn't for him. He'd also told her about Isadora's birth and for months, she wouldn't even speak to him. But then she'd mellowed and their marriage was on its way to mending when this happened.

He was aware that many of his peers also had baseborn children who they shunted off to orphanages or boarding schools so their wives would never know about their indiscretions. But he just couldn't do it to this child, who had always been so happy to see him whenever he visited. It was because of her that he'd continued keeping Rita in the high life to which he'd introduced her. He had hoped that she would settle down and take good care of the child.

Sadly, she was like one of those flighty birds which can never be tamed no matter how hard man tries. At the first taste of freedom, they're gone.

"Papa?"

"Yes, Isadora?"

"Will I like it where you're taking me and will you come to visit me?" He gave her a stricken look. "Mama said that one day when she's not there, you would come and take me to a place where they look after children who have no mothers," the way Isadora said it so casually made Edgar realise that there was so much Rita must have told her.

"We're going to my house where I live," he said.

"Why?" She seemed genuinely puzzled. "Mama said we can never come to live with you." Isadora had asked her mother the question why they didn't live with her father and the first response she got was a resounding slap and the stern warning to never ask that again. But after a while, her mother had calmed down and explained that her father didn't want them to live with him because he had another family. "What will your other family say?"

"Oh dear!" Edgar sighed to himself. He had no idea what Rita had told the child for eight years and he wondered if he was doing the right thing by bringing Isadora to his home. Maybe, like his peers, he should just have found her a good orphanage or boarding school and supported her until she became an adult.

Isadora was an outspoken child and Clarissa wouldn't like that at all. What had he done?

2

DREAMER IN THE VALLEY

Isadora stopped at the end of the snowy driveway and glanced back toward the house. She was running away and wasn't going to come back to this house where she wasn't wanted. Dashing away the tears from her eyes, she picked up her small bag, only to come face to face with her half-brother, Arthur.

"Where do you think you're going?"

"Get out of my way, Arthur," she flashed angry eyes at him.

"I don't think you're going anywhere, at least not in this kind of weather."

"Get away from me," she tried to side step him but he blocked her. "Just leave me be," she started crying again.

"Things can't be that bad, Isadora."

"Mama was right," she said, letting the tears flow. "Papa didn't want us to live with him and he doesn't want me."

"That's not true," Arthur was worried. He had to get Isadora back to the house because the weather was changing very fast and any time now the skies would open and they would be drenched by snow. "Papa wants you and that's why he brought you here."

Isadora snorted and turned her face away. She'd been searching for Arthur that morning when she heard loud voices coming from her father's study. It was her father and stepmother and they were having a terrible row.

"Why did you have to go and bring that harlot's seed into this house to taint our family?"

"Clarissa, the child has no one else and I'm the only father she's known since she was born."

"That's what you think. What makes you believe that she is your actual child?"

"Because Rita told me that she's my daughter."

"And you believed the word of a harlot? Edgar, what's come over you? We were doing so well as a family and then you had to go and bring that evil seed into our home. You can be sure of one thing, don't expect me to treat her like a child of the house."

"And what does that mean?"

"The sooner she learns that this isn't her permanent home, the better for her."

"Isadora belongs with us, Clarissa."

"If you want peace in this household, Edgar, you will leave me be and let me do what I want to do as the mistress of this house. Don't interfere in my ways and I'll leave you well alone. I should never have trusted you when you said you were finished with that woman. Now you've brought her child into my home and expect me to be alright with it?"

"She's just a child and I will make sure she stays out of your way."

"The best thing you can do is get her out of this house, Edgar."

"That's not possible because I can't just throw my daughter away."

"So now she's better than Arthur?"

"Woman, would you stop putting words into my mouth? Arthur is my son and first born but it wasn't fine for him to be an only child. Remember that you couldn't have more children after he was born."

"So now it's my fault and because I couldn't have more children that you decided to go and find a woman from the gutters and sire a child with her?"

"Clarissa!"

"I'm tired of this conversation because you've clearly made up your mind that she is staying. But let's get one thing clear, she's not my daughter and I will never accept her as such. If I ever get the chance to get her out of our lives, believe me, I will take it."

"Isadora, let's go home," Arthur tried to take her hand but she pulled away. "It will soon start snowing and you're not even dressed for the weather."

"I don't care," she said. "Just let me go," she was screaming now.

"What's happening here, Arthur?" Arthur turned to find the vicar walking toward them. "Why is this child screaming and who is she?"

"She's my sister, Isadora," Arthur said. "Papa brought her home two weeks ago but I found her trying to run away. She says no one wants her but that's not true."

"Little one," Reverend George Simms turned to Isadora and held out a hand. "My name is George Simms and I'm the vicar of this parish. What is wrong?"

"Nothing," she felt frightened because apart from her father, she'd never been this close to a grown up man before. Her mother had told her that grown up men weren't good and they could hurt her. That was the reason Rita would always tell her to hide whenever her male visitors would come to the house.

"You can't say that nothing is wrong when you're crying and carrying your bag. Why don't you come to my house so that my wife can make us all something hot to drink and chase away the cold?"

Isadora looked up at her brother, who nodded. "Let's go and see Mrs. Salome," he told her. "She always bakes delicious cinnamon and honey buns and cookies. I bet you will want to eat a whole tin of them."

Isadora giggled, "No one can eat a whole tin of buns," she wiped the tears away with the back of her hands.

"Oh, but you wait and see," Arthur said, giving the vicar a grateful look. "They're so delicious that you will want to eat all of them."

"And Arthur is right. Mrs. Salome just removed a fresh batch of cookies from the oven and if you hurry, she will let you lick the batter tin before she washes it."

All thoughts of running away fled from Isadora's mind as she took her brother's hand and skipped happily beside him. Arthur easily picked her bag up and she grinned up at him. He was strong and always made her feel safe, even though he was only thirteen. To her, he was big and brave and she never felt scared whenever she was with him. If he thought the vicar was a good person then he must be right.

3

THE BOND HUSBAND

It was nearly midnight, and Edgar was staring unseeingly into the night. He'd planned to go to bed early and rest but instead, he'd walked in to find his wife yelling at Isadora. Her attitude troubled him because the child wasn't as bad as Clarissa made her out to be, but for the sake of peace in the home, he never said much.

He was aware that behind his back, all his servants called him a henpecked husband or "Mr. Yes Dear," which was what he always said whenever he wanted to end an argument with Clarissa.

The study door opened and he found Arthur standing there. "Why aren't you in bed?"

"Papa, I heard Isadora crying. What's wrong?"

Edgar sighed and walked to his son. "Your sister is very sensitive and she had a few words with your mother. They're both very upset and I told Isadora to go to her room for a while."

"Did you hit her?"

"Arthur! You know that I would never hit Isadora."

"I don't like seeing Isadora sad."

"I know that, son. But she is also growing up and has to be corrected whenever she is wrong."

"Just don't cane her, Papa."

"Why don't you go back to bed? I'll see you in the morning."

"Yes, Pa."

But Arthur didn't go back to his bedroom. He was really troubled because Isadora had been in this house for two years now and yet she kept threatening to run away one day. The thought of her going out into the world alone frightened him. At fifteen, he already knew the evils that lurked everywhere especially in as far as girls were concerned.

His father had told him that he would be going to Eton but he didn't want to leave Isadora alone with his mother. One of the servants, Hubert the stable man had told him why his mother was so angry with Isadora all the time.

"You've got to understand that it's not easy for your mother, boy," Hubert had said in response to his question.

"Why?"

"Isadora is a reminder that your father had er..." the man coughed, clearly uncomfortable at sharing the information with the young boy.

"Hubert, I'm no longer a child and I know that many men keep mistresses."

"Well, just as you said, you father had a mistress but that was a long time ago and it didn't go down well with your mother. She hated the child's mother even without ever meeting her. Even though the woman is now dead and the relationship between her and your father ended years ago, the pain of knowing that she was once there and that she bore a child for your father is too much for your mother to bear."

"But Isadora didn't ask to be born."

"You're a good boy for defending your sister, but all that is adult stuff and you shouldn't be worrying your head about it. If you want to help your mother and sister at the same time, you will keep them away from each other.

That little minx is high spirited and seems to have a mouth bigger than her head. In this household, that will get her into a lot of trouble."

"I'll do my best," he had promised but apparently once again, he'd failed. It was true that Isadora was very high spirited and spoke her mind without thinking. But she was ten and just a child and he felt that she shouldn't be so severely reprimanded.

"Why are you still up?" His mother's voice startled him. "Go to your room at once and I don't want you wandering around the hallway in darkness. You could fall and hurt yourself."

"Yes, Ma," he said, hurrying to his bedchamber. He would find Isadora in the morning and comfort her.

4

DARK NIGHT

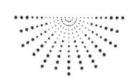

Isadora had just turned eleven when something happened that frightened her to the core. She woke up to a searing pain in her lower abdomen and when she stepped out of bed, noticed that the sheets and her night dress had droplets of blood. She screamed and Hilda, one of their maids ran into the room. The girl had been dusting the banister when she heard Isadora cry out. Like all the other servants, Hilda treated Isadora well because she was such a sweet child. They also felt sorry for her because of the way Clarissa treated her but no one could say a word for fear of losing their jobs.

"Isadora, what's wrong?"

All the child could do was point at the bed. "Someone cut me," she sobbed. "And my stomach is killing me."

To her surprise, Hilda threw her head back and laughed, then took her hand and led her back to the bed. "Little Isadora, this means that you're now a big girl."

"What?" Isadora frowned.

"No one cut you and what you're going through is something that happens to all women when they get to about your age. It is God's monthly gift to women all over the world."

"Why should the gift bring pain then?"

"Oh dear child, don't see it as pain but as a sign that you are a normal young woman now. I'll bring you something to drink that will help with the pain. Do you want to get back into bed?" Isadora nodded. "Then let me cover you up while I fetch you the drink. When you're feeling better, I'll come and help you change the sheets and show you what you must do so that you don't bring shame to yourself and others."

Her words made no sense but it was a relief to know that she wasn't dying. The pain was excruciating and she curled into a fetal position, her hand pressing against her abdomen.

"What are you still doing in bed?" her stepmother's voice came from across the room. "You're nothing but a lazy and good for nothing girl. Get out of bed this instant."

Isadora knew better than argue with the woman and so she struggled to get out of her bed but bent over double as another wave of pain overtook her.

"Stand up straight," Clarissa ordered.

"I can't," Isadora was sobbing now. "My stomach hurts so bad."

Hilda entered the room and took in the situation with a glance and then retreated. Good thing Clarissa's back was turned toward her so her mistress didn't see her. The last thing she wanted was to get into any kind of battle of words with the irate woman. She ran into Arthur as she was going back down the stairs.

"Here," she thrust the small pitcher in his hands. "Take that to Isadora and make sure she drinks it."

"What?" He turned around to ask her what it was but she had fled and disappeared into the kitchen. He'd been about to leave the house when he heard his mother shouting and knew that it had to do with Isadora. So he hurried to the bedroom and was surprised to find Isadora kneeling on the floor, clutching her stomach. "Mother, what did you do?"

"Stay out of this, Arthur," Clarissa gave him a harsh glare. "It's nearly eight and I found this one lounging in the bed like a lazy lout."

"Can't you see that she's not well, Mother?" He glared at her in turn. "Isadora, get back into bed."

"Are you now teaching this girl to be insubordinate to me?"

"Mother, look at her," Arthur placed the pitcher on the small bedside table. "She is clearly ill and needs medicine. Hilda gave me this stuff to help her."

"I see that this house now belongs to Isadora," Clarissa clicked and then turned and left the room.

"Arthur, please go and say sorry to your mother. I'll be alright," Isadora said in a strained voice.

"No, I'm not leaving you when you're like this."

"Please," she started crying because she didn't want him to see the stains on her sheets and on her nightdress. She was feeling embarrassed at being caught like this. "Please go."

"Are you sure you'll be alright?"

"Yes."

"At least let me help you get into bed."

"No," she screamed and he took a step backwards. "Leave me alone, I don't need any more trouble. Just go," she shouted.

Arthur left, closing the door behind him but he stood there for a while not believing that Isadora hadn't wanted him to help her. What was wrong with her that she didn't want him in her bedroom?

~

She was in bed for two days before the pain finally subsided and she could get up again. Hilda came and helped her through the dark nights, rubbing her back and even bringing her a hot stone wrapped in linens.

"This will ease the pain a little bit."

"Will it always be like this?" Isadora asked in a small voice.

"Not always, but it's good to be prepared at all times. If you take the medicine I give you before your monthly present comes, then it won't be so bad."

"Do men also get the monthly present from God?"

Hilda laughed, "Isadora, you ask the funniest questions. No, men don't get what we women get. That is what makes us all different. And Isadora, you now have to be very careful."

"About what?"

"Like I told you the other day, you're now a big girl and if you do something wrong, then you will have a baby."

Isadora gave the maid a blank stare. What was this woman talking about? "You mean if I steal an apple from the pantry or candy from the drawer then I'll have a baby?'

Hilda shook her head, "I mean, you have to be very careful around men now. Don't let any of them take liberties with you."

"What do you mean by liberties?"

"Isadora, I don't know how to say it. Didn't your mother teach you the things that go on between men and women?"

Isadora shook her head, "Mama is dead and she didn't tell me anything."

"Well, just be careful about what you do. Don't ever let a man lift your skirts up."

"Why would anyone want to do that?"

Hilda was clearly at a loss of words but before she could think of a suitable reply, heard a bell tinkling somewhere in the house. "Mrs. Clarissa needs me," she looked relieved and Isadora watched her leave, a puzzled look in her eyes.

Then her face brightened. She would ask Arthur to explain to her what Hilda had been telling her. Grownups were so difficult to understand but Arthur was clever and knew everything.

She found him reading in the drawing room. "Arthur, can I ask you something?"

"Sure," he looked up and smiled at her and she felt funny in her stomach. His dark eyes were so intense and she had started feeling shy around him. "What's on your mind, little Isadora?"

"Hilda told me that I should never let a man lift my skirts up," she looked down at her round frock. "Why would anyone want to lift my skirts up?"

Arthur felt himself turning red. For a while now, he'd been trying to find a way of telling Isadora that he didn't like it when she played in the stables while the other young men were there. They had started teasing her but in her innocence she didn't think they were up to any funny tricks. She had no idea just how beautiful she was and he'd overheard one of the stable boys referring to her as a graceful swan.

"What's wrong, Arthur?"

"Isadora, Hilda was trying to tell you that you need to stop going to the stables when you're alone. If you want to ride then ask me and I'll take you but don't go into the stables alone."

"Why?"

What could he tell her to get through to her? "Look, it's dangerous to be around young men and I want you to promise me that you'll never go to the stables alone." He looked really fierce and Isadora was a little frightened. "Promise me that, Isadora," he held her by the shoulders and shook her slightly. "Promise me."

"I promise," she said in a trembling voice, her eyes filling with tears. She'd done something to anger Arthur and he was the last person she ever wanted to offend. "I'm sorry."

"Oh Isadora," he wiped the tears away. "I'm sorry for sounding really harsh but I only care about you and don't want anything bad to happen to you."

"I promise."

"Good. Now wipe those tears away then go and put on your coat. I'll take you down to the village square and get you some candy and a nice trinket."

"Oh Arthur," she threw her arms around him, "You're the best brother anyone could ask for and I love you so much."

Her words pleased him and he smiled as he watched her rushing out of the drawing room.

∽

From the cover of the trees on the far side of the road, Isadora watched her stepmother and father as they drove away in the fancy family carriage. This particular carriage was one of four that the family owned and it was only used on those occasions when her parents were visiting one of their wealthy neighbours. She felt guilty spying on them but she had nothing else to do. They were headed to a ball on the other side of the village and she'd wanted to see how flashy they looked in their fancy new clothes. Arthur was also supposed to go with them but he'd declined at the last moment and she knew it was because of Margaret Piper their neighbour.

Maggie, as she told everyone to call her, was fifteen and liked flirting with Arthur. It often made Isadora angry but she could see that her brother enjoyed the attention. And it wasn't only Maggie who liked coming by the house, many other young women would visit them from time to time and Clarissa didn't seem to mind. But Papa always frowned when he saw the girls and heard them giggling in the drawing room.

Isadora was hiding out in the trees because Maggie was at the house and Arthur was holding her hand. She'd seen them cosy up to each other and gotten so angry that she'd run out of the house.

A twig snapped causing her to quickly turn around, then she smiled when she saw who it was.

"Isadora, what are you doing skulking out here in the woods? Don't you know that an insect might bite you?"

"Mrs. Salome, I just wanted to watch Pa and my stepmother driving away in the fancy carriage."

"You could as well have done that from the windows of the house," the woman held a hand out. "Come, I can see that something else is troubling you. Tell me and let's see if I can help you deal with it."

Isadora pouted, "It's that Piper girl," she growled and because she was looking down, didn't see the amusement on the older woman's face.

"Oh, so you all have a visitor now and you don't like her."

"She is always coming to the house, giggling like a silly idiot and then holding Arthur's hand."

"How does that make you feel?"

"I don't like it," Isadora said honestly.

"Why? Arthur is growing up and the ladies are now noticing him. It won't be long before he has to take a wife and start a family. He's sixteen now and most young men his age begin looking for brides at this time. But don't worry, I don't think he will get married just yet, but you've got to understand that it's all part of growing up."

"Well, I don't like growing up," Isadora said with a deep scowl on her brow. "Growing up is bothersome."

"You'll understand more when you're older, child. One day, you'll also want to hold hands with a boy and smile and giggle like a silly idiot, just like Maggie Piper is doing with your brother."

"No," Isadora said hotly. "I won't let a boy hold my hand," she felt angry just thinking about it. There was only one person who she liked holding her hand and right now, he was back in the house holding the hand of some silly scatter-brained female.

Salome Simms was wise and knew that the girl still had a lot to understand before she came to the realisation that flirting was part of human nature.

"Come, I just made some cranberry jam, why don't you come and get one jar and take it back home with you?"

5

JUST AN ILLUSION

Christmas was promising to be a truly glorious day. It was her twelfth one and she could barely sit still because it was also her birthday.

Isadora had woken up to the rare December sunshine and according to her, it was going to be the best day of her life.

"You look really happy," she met Arthur on the landing and they walked down the stairs together, holding hands and grinning like little children.

"Oh Arthur," Isadora danced by his side, "You know how much I love Christmas which is also my birthday. And this year, I think Papa bought us really nice presents."

"We can go and take a peek at them," Arthur suggested, feeling really happy. He loved spending time with Isadora because she was always so bright and cheerful, well, most of the time anyway.

"And where do the two of you think you're going?" Clarissa's voice stopped them both in their tracks and they turned to watch her as she walked down the stairs. "You're making so much noise and it's still early in the morning."

"Ma, its Christmas Day."

"Arthur, I wasn't talking to you."

"I'm sorry, Mama," Isadora lowered her head. She just hoped her stepmother wouldn't tell her to stay in the bedroom and miss out on the festivities. Her father came up behind her stepmother.

"Clarissa, leave the children be. It's Christmas Day and also Isadora's birthday and they have the right to be happy."

To Isadora's relief, Clarissa mumbled something unintelligible and flounced toward the kitchen, no doubt to bother the staff. She didn't envy them one bit and felt sorry that their day would probably be ruined by her stepmother's bad mood.

"Let's go," Arthur said in an excited voice and they rushed to the living room and to the Christmas tree where there were a number of wrapped presents for them.

This year, she had saved the pennies which her father gave her from time to time and bought Arthur a book. Gulliver's Travels written by Jonathan Swift was the book she'd chosen to give her brother as his Christmas present, and then she also painted him a picture of a bird in flight.

"These are for you," she held out the gifts to him, feeling shy at his intense gaze.

"These look very good," Arthur quickly tore the wrapping paper and then smiled. "You got me Gulliver's Travels, how did you find it?"

Isadora glowed at the joy she saw on Arthur's face. "I asked Vicar Simms to get it for me when he went to London. Do you like it?"

"Like it, I love it, thank you so much, Isadora," he said. "Now it makes my own gift pale in comparison."

"Let me see, let me see," she chanted, holding out her hands. Arthur placed a small box in it. "This is a bracelet that I found and thought it reminded me of you. It's made of small precious stones."

Isadora wasn't listening. She quickly opened the box and pulled the bracelet out. "It's beautiful, thank you so much, Arthur."

"That's for your birthday and this," he held out a pretty multicoloured scarf. "This one is your Christmas present."

"I love them both so much," she hugged him and was surprised when he quickly pulled away. "Sorry," she frowned then turned to her presents. "I promise that I will wear them all the time," she indicated the gifts.

Arthur stared at the picture she'd painted for him. Even though she wasn't all that good a painter, he felt touched that she'd taken the time to do it. The colourful bird reminded him of Isadora and her cheerfulness. "And thank you for my gifts too, Isadora," he touched her cheek. "I'll treasure them for the rest of my life."

∼

After a heavy meal, Isadora was feeling drowsy and happy. For once, her stepmother wasn't screaming at her. It had indeed been a wonderful day and she raised her hand to look at the bracelet that Arthur had given her.

"If you keep staring at it, it will lose all its colours," he teased her.

She made a face at him and followed him to his bedroom where he told her he wanted to read the book she had given him. "Come, let's read it together," he made room for her on his large bed and she needed no second bidding. "So that we don't fall asleep, we'll each read a paragraph. Isadora," he tried to shake her but she had fallen into deep sleep. "Isadora, wake up," he tried again but the girl was gone into dreamland.

With a sigh, he started reading but didn't get farther than the first page and was soon asleep, his arm around Isadora.

~

The loud banging and shouting woke the youngsters and they jumped up. "What are you doing?" Clarissa was screaming like a banshee. "Woe is me, woe is me for my eyes have beheld an evil so great upon the earth that I will be blinded," she was beating her chest as she said this. "What is this you have done?"

Edgar chose to come into the bedroom at that moment. "Clarissa, what is going on?"

"Ask them," she pointed at Arthur and Isadora. "An abomination has occurred under our very roof. I warned you that this would happen but you didn't listen, now it has happened."

"What has happened?"

"Ask them," she screamed, "I found your daughter laying in sin with our son. An abomination has occurred in this house."

"Papa, we didn't do anything," Arthur turned red when his father fixed his eyes on him. "We were just reading the book that Isadora got me when we fell asleep."

"It's true," Isadora said in a shaky voice. She'd never seen her father look so angry but it was more than that. There was a look of disgust and loathing on his face and she couldn't bear it. "I'm sorry, it won't happen again," and she stood there trembling.

Edgar didn't say a word but left the room. Clarissa turned to the two children, "You want to bring shame and a cursed child into this world?" She hissed at them. "Get down to the study, both of you." They practically ran there and once inside, she shut the door. "You've been a very badly behaved girl, Isadora," she went behind the large desk and brought out a long cane. "I have to teach you how to behave like a lady," she said. "Now, lie down at once." Isadora obeyed and sobbed in anguish as the lashes fell on her back. "Get out of my sight, you cursed child," her stepmother hauled her to her feet and pushed her out the door.

Isadora didn't immediately go to her room but stood at the door listening to hear if Arthur would be punished as she had been. Nothing of the sort happened. Instead, Clarissa just gave him a mild scolding. That really angered Isadora because not once did Arthur try to defend her to his mother. He simply kept his mouth shut. When she realised that they were about to come out of the study, Isadora ran to her bedroom and climbed onto her bed, sobbing because she had a feeling that something terrible was about to happen.

∼

The days after Christmas Day were dreadful. The household was solemn and the New Year was ushered in without the customary pomp. No one was in the mood to celebrate because her father had left on Christmas Day and didn't return.

She was seated in her bedroom when she heard a wail come from downstairs. Her heart skipped a beat and she went out to find out what was going on.

"You," her stepmother pointed at her when she caught sight of her on the landing. "Come down here at once," and Isadora obeyed, trembling as she descended the stairs. "You brought a curse on this family," the woman screamed. "Now my husband is dead because of your wickedness. You sent him out of the house and he went and met his death."

"Mama, is it true?" Arthur emerged from the study. "Is Papa dead?"

"Yes. He left home because he couldn't bear to look at the two of you and especially this devil's seed that he brought into this house from the gutters."

"Don't say that."

"It's true. I warned your father that this would happen but he wouldn't listen and now he's dead."

∽

Since Edgar's body wasn't recovered, a requiem mass was said for him but there was no burial even though Clarissa asked for one. Arthur stood firm and said they weren't going to bury an empty coffin.

Isadora hadn't stopped sobbing from the moment the news of her father's death came. What was worse was that it was all her fault that he had left home. She shouldn't have slept on her brother's bed. It was all her fault.

As soon as the service was over and they went back into the house, Clarissa turned to her, "In the study, right now. Not you," she snarled at Arthur when he would have followed them. Once they got into the study, Clarissa got out a belt and raised it. "You've been a bad girl and deserve this punishment. You're no longer welcome in this house. I never wanted you here in the first place. With your father gone, any obligation I had toward you is also gone."

"I'm sorry," Isadora sobbed.

"That's not good enough. I warned my husband that you were nothing but trouble and I was proved right." She had an ugly expression on her face that frightened Isadora and she brought down the belt, catching her off guard. She screamed at the pain as the belt landed across her face. "You're just as bad as your filthy mother and you are lucky that my husband even accepted you. You mother was one of the worst women in England, and you were never a child of this house." Down came the belt again and this time it landed at the back of Isadora's head.

"Your mother gave her favours to any man who had two pence to rub together and I'm sure men streamed in and out of your house at all hours of the day," Isadora gave a small cry because what her stepmother was saying was right. She had seen men troop in and out of their house at all hours of the day and her mother had said they were her visitors. But now that she thought about it and with what she'd learned over the past four years, she now knew that her mother had sold her favours to men for money. It was true, her mother had been a harlot, a woman of the night.

But Clarissa wasn't done with the girl. "You have your mother's blood in you, a harlot's blood and it's just a matter of time before you start giving yourself to men for money. You have even started doing it right under my own roof."

"We didn't do anything," Isadora sobbed.

"Be quiet," the belt landed across her back. "Don't talk back at me, you worthless girl. You know what you've done? An abomination is what it is and you will burn in hell. God will never forgive you. You're actually better off dead and now that my husband is gone, there's no need for you to remain in this household anymore."

6

MAIDEN'S PENANCE

"I'm sorry, I promise I'll be good," Isadora sobbed as the carriage drove down the driveway and out of sight of the house in the deep of the night.

"You shut up now," a voice she didn't recognize hissed at her. "Mrs. Fontaine wants you gone out of her home forever and this is what your life will be from now on."

Earlier that day, Isadora had thought her troubles were over when she was sent up to her bedchamber after receiving the whipping of her life. But then in the middle of the night, she was woken up roughly. *"You're getting out of this house," her stepmother hissed. "I've had enough trouble with you and no more."*

"Where are you taking me?" She'd asked in a small voice.

"That's none of your concern. But after today, you will no longer be my problem."

And just like that, she was whisked out of the house, pushed into a carriage and off they went. She cried herself to sleep all the way and didn't know when they got to their destination or how long they had been travelling.

"Wake up," she was pushed roughly off the seat and landed on the floor of the carriage. "Get out right now."

"Where are we?" Isadora was really frightened. The place was dark and all she could make out in the moonlit night were tall buildings that seemed to want to swallow her up.

"Get moving," she was pushed forward and soon found herself inside what seemed to be a large hallway. There were gas lamps placed along the walls and she could see that it was something like a school. It was not long before she realised that she was at a workhouse of sorts.

Another woman came down the corridor. "Get this girl to the dormitory at once," Isadora's traveling companion growled.

"Yes, Miss Rebecca ," the lady stuttered, clearly intimidated by the woman standing before them.

"Come with me," but her tone was gentler and she led the way, leaving Isadora to follow her. They must have walked forever before they got to an old door. "This place was built in the sixteenth century," she was saying. "It was actually a monastery for over two hundred years before, but it fell into disrepair and was turned into a workhouse laundry. You'll be happy here," she smiled as she let Isadora precede her into what seemed to be a room full of wood but they turned out to be beds. "Don't make noise to awaken the others. I'll come and get you in the morning."

~

Arthur felt heavy when he woke up. It felt as though someone had played drums in his head while he slept and he woke up with a dry mouth.

The moment he went downstairs, he knew something was wrong. "Hilda, what's going on?"

The maid merely gave him a cold look and then walked back to the kitchen. The other servants quickly moved out of the way when they saw him coming. He wondered why Isadora hadn't come searching for him as was her custom, then he remembered that in the past few days, she'd been very distant from him and he couldn't blame her.

On Christmas Day, he hadn't stepped forward to defend her as he ought to and she got punished. He knew because he'd witnessed the caning in his father's study and hadn't done anything to stop it. Isadora wouldn't even speak or look at him after that and he felt crushed. He missed her and the past week had been terrible for all of them. His father was dead and gone and now the only other person he truly loved was absent.

She was probably in the bedroom and he climbed the stairs once again. But her room was empty and the bed had been stripped. What was going on in this household?

"Mother," he came down the stairs once again.

"Oh, there you are, Arthur," Clarissa looked pale. "Isadora ran away in the deep of the night. We have searched high and low but there's not a single trace of the girl."

"No," Arthur shook his head. "I don't believe you."

"Arthur, listen to me," his mother took his hands. "Isadora was a troubled child and after what happened, she must have felt deep shame."

"That's just it," he snatched his hands away and glared at her. "You hated Isadora from the moment she set foot in this house and wanted her gone. With Papa dead, you got your chance and are now pretending that she has run away."

"Don't you dare speak to me like that," his mother gave him a hard slap but he didn't even flinch. "I'm sorry," she tried to reach out but he stepped aside. "I didn't mean to do that."

"No matter what you do, I'm going to search until I find Isadora and bring her back to this house."

"Son, I'm sorry."

He gave her a cold look before turning his back on her and walking away. He had to find Isadora and the first place he headed to was the vicar's house. Many times when things were difficult at home, she would go and visit with Salome Simms.

The vicar opened the door for him. "My boy, it's just too early in the morning for a visit, what are you doing here?"

"Is Isadora here?" His eyes quickly darted around the room. Salome emerged from the kitchen carrying a tray. "Mrs. Salome, is Isadora in the kitchen with you?"

She shook her head, "No, we haven't seen her since yesterday afternoon. Is there a problem?"

"Yes, my mother says she ran away at night but I don't believe her."

"Where would she go that late and what made her leave home?" The vicar fixed his eyes on the young man. "Arthur, if you don't tell me what's going on then how do you expect us to help you?"

"It started a few days ago," and he went on to tell them what had happened on Christmas Day. "But we weren't doing anything wrong. Isadora fell asleep on my bed and I was reading and also dozed off. My mother found us and said we had done wrong." He shook his head, "I should have spoken up and defended Isadora but I didn't."

"So what happened?"

"Ma caned Isadora after Papa left. That was the last time we saw him alive until we received the news that he had died. Yesterday when we returned from the requiem service, Mama took the cane to Isadora and I just stood there," he bowed his head in shame. "She then sent Isadora to her bedroom but this morning when I woke up, I found that Isadora was missing and my mother said she had run away."

"Did she leave a note to that effect?"

"If she did, I didn't see it and my mother didn't show it to me. I just know that something bad has happened to Isadora and it's all my fault."

"Don't blame yourself," the vicar looked at the distraught young man. "She is probably hiding out somewhere and waiting for things to calm down at home."

"The servants went as far as the village square to search for her but no one has seen her. She seems to have just dropped off the face of the earth and I'm really worried. What if someone abducted her and has taken her to Liverpool to sell her off to become someone's slave?"

"You're rushing to think the worst when there is probably a good explanation. Just calm down and we'll all help you to find Isadora. I don't think she could have gone very far especially not if she was on foot."

"What have I done," he whispered hoarsely. "Why didn't I defend Isadora when I had the chance to do so?"

"Why didn't you defend her if she was innocent?"

"Because..." he twisted his lips and turned away, feeling the heat creeping up his neck. "When Isadora fell asleep, I watched her for a little while. She looked so peaceful and beautiful lying there and I wanted to kiss her." There, it was out and he felt such deep shame. "She's only a child and more than that, she's my half sister but I found myself wanting to kiss her on the lips."

7

THE FORGOTTEN PATH

Isadora cried all night every night. Her good life had ended and she was now nothing more than a slave in this seemingly God forsaken place. She wasn't allowed to attend classes with the other girls but had to work every hour. St. Magdalene's Laundry was large and housed about two hundred girls and fifteen other women supposedly employed to take care of them. Occasionally the owner of the workhouse would make an appearance, but his visits were rare. The lady in charge, Rebecca, was fearsome and ruthless. The only man in the laundry was her nephew, and sadly he was not a good one.

She'd been here for a month now and in all that time, she'd been thinking how she might run away. But where would she go now that her father was dead and her stepmother didn't want her at home? Maybe Vicar George and his wife could take her in but they had five children and their house was small. Besides, living in the same parish as her stepmother would only be courting trouble.

And another thing, she never wanted to see Arthur again because as far as she was concerned, he had betrayed her. He had always promised that he would protect her but when it had counted most, he'd kept silent as she bore the punishment for something she didn't do. But yet everyone said she had committed a terrible sin and would never find absolution, not in this life nor in the next.

Every day she was relentlessly reminded by Rebecca why she was here. *"You committed an abomination and there can be no mercy for your kind. Maybe if you work hard enough, dear girl, God will see fit to have mercy on your sorry soul!"* It was almost as if she relished the torment little Isadora toiled under.

To a twelve-year-old child those words left a deep impression on her mind and fear in her heart. She didn't want to go and burn in hell and if working her fingers to the bone behind these dark walls could keep her out of those raging fires then she would do so for the rest of her life.

Isadora determined to make amends somehow for her father's death, rising before the other girls to pray in the small chapel that the nearby church had paid to be built on the workhouse grounds, right next to the existing workhouse buildings, believing some of the lost souls punished behind its walls might somehow find salvation. Despite the church being just a stone throw from the workhouse, many of the people there were denied the joy of an hour of worship. Work, it seemed, was more important than worship, although the laundry denied ever compelling its residents to work on the Lord's day. In the end, the church decided that if the house would not come to them, they would take the church to the house.

Father O'Connor faithfully tended the chapel, and sometimes Isadora would often see him there in the pre-dawn hours.

One morning at exactly four o'clock, she was up and out of her bed. "Where are you going?" Martha the girl who slept in the bed above hers asked. "It's still very dark." Martha was one of the girls who spoke to Isadora. The others treated her like a leper and she knew that it was because Rebecca had told them to do so.

"Martha, go to sleep," Isadora didn't want to disturb any of the other girls. "I just need to use the outhouse."

"I'll come with you," Martha was out of the bed before Isadora could stop her. "I wanted to go but was afraid because it's so dark and I'm scared of going out there all by myself."

Seeing that there was no way she could stop her friend from coming with her, she nodded and the two of them slipped out of the dormitory.

"Sometimes I feel afraid that this door isn't strong enough to protect us if someone were to break in and try to hurt us," Martha whispered. "These people don't care about us."

"Ssh! Don't ever let anyone hear you saying that or you could get into a lot of trouble."

"Why are we going to the chapel?" Martha noticed that they weren't taking their usual route to the outhouses on the other side of the dormitory. The darkness was frightening but solitary lamps kept the corridors somewhat lit. Still, the shadows cast made Isadora's heart beat very fast. She always thought that people were lurking in the shadows watching her. Even though she didn't want to show it, she was glad Martha had decided to come along. "Isadora, this isn't a direct route to the outhouses."

"It's easier to access the outhouses from this side and the lamps also light up the path instead of us walking in darkness."

They walked swiftly and silently and soon got to the outhouses. Once they were done, Isadora turned to Martha. "You can go back to bed now."

"What are you waiting for?"

"Nothing, I just need to go into the chapel to pray."

"At this time? Even a nun wouldn't come to pray this early."

"Martha, please don't ask me questions, just go back to the dorm," she said and turned to walk away. On this particular morning, the old priest, Father O'Connor was mumbling at the altar. He was half blind and so relied more on his other senses. The girls always said that he had sharp ears and could hear a feather drop to the ground.

"Who's there?" he called out.

"Father O'Connor, it's just me," Isadora called out.

"What do you want, child?"

"To say my prayers as I do every day." Whenever Isadora saw him, he always asked her the same question and she gave him the same response. Isadora felt uncomfortable because Martha hadn't gone back to the dormitory but had followed her to the chapel.

"Very well then, carry on," the priest continued arranging the items on the altar for mass. Isadora wondered why the old priest saw the need to do that by himself when he easily could have someone do it for him. She rarely found anyone else in the chapel at this early hour, other than the aging, and sleepless, Father O'Connor.

Isadora expected Martha to leave but she followed her to one of the pews. "Why are you following me, Martha?"

"You're strange," Martha said. "I've been watching you for a while and just wanted to know what you're up to."

"I come here to pray," Isadora sat down and chose to ignore her friend. Isadora bowed her head hoping that Martha would leave. An hour later, Isadora hadn't said any prayers and she wanted to cry. Why had Martha insisted on sitting with her? What if her missing prayer on this day counted against her?

What was she going to do? Then she brightened up, tomorrow she would come in an hour earlier and compensate for missing today's session. Maybe God would see her sacrifice and consider forgiving her.

"We have to go now or we'll be in big trouble," she whispered as she slipped out of the pew.

"Where are we going?" Martha ran to catch up with her.

"You back to the dorm, me to start my day's work."

The next day Isadora rose at 3am.

8

THE DARK RAINBOW

The church bells wouldn't stop tolling and Isadora groaned as she tried to cover her head with the pillow to shut the sound out. Incessant ringing could only mean one thing; that someone had died. Usually it was one of the older workers in the place, since there were quite a number of people who had sadly ended up here and toiled away the final years of their life.

"I just wish it would stop," Martha said from the bed above. "Why do they have to keep ringing so loud?"

"Someone must be dead," Isadora answered. "They only sound like that when a death has occurred."

"Who do you think it is?" Another girl called out from across the dorm.

"I have no idea, maybe its old Rhoda. She's the oldest here and I think she has finally gone."

"Or it could be Monica. She's been very sick and maybe she's the one who has died."

One by one, the girls talked and speculated about the person most likely to have died. But when morning came, they found out that it was the old priest who had died. He'd been praying in the chapel when he fell and lay there the whole night. By the time someone found him, he was already dead.

"Miss Rebecca wants to see you right now," Marcie said, Isadora was dragged from her work station. "And she's in a foul mood," she shook her head and Isadora could see the pity in her eyes. "I don't know what you did this time child, but I fear for you."

Isadora wondered what she had done wrong this time and was soon to find out. "Did you go for your prayers today?"

"H-how do you know I go for prayer?"

"I know everything that happens in this place, you silly child. Now tell me plainly, how is it that you didn't see Father O'Connor as he lay dying on the altar floor? Are you lying to me?"

"No. I swear I didn't see Father O'Connor because he wasn't there this morning."

"That's because he'd fallen, you stupid girl. Why didn't you check around for him?" Isadora longed to tell her accuser that it wasn't her responsibility to check on the old priest but held her peace. The last thing she wanted was a flogging. It was too cold for that.

"I'm sorry," she said instead, looking down at the floor.

"Look at me," the woman hissed. "You're nothing but trouble and I'm sure you saw the priest but since you are evil, and you wanted him dead."

"That's not true, I didn't see him when I went to the chapel to pray."

"Get out of my sight before I kick you." And Isadora fled.

~

Two days later, there was much excitement in the workhouse and among the girls and Isadora wondered why.

"What's going on?" She asked Martha whose face was ablaze with excitement. "Why is everyone so excited all of a sudden?"

"Did you see him?"

"See who?"

"The new priest, Father John."

She wondered why everyone would be all excited because of an elderly priest.

"You've got to see him to understand why we're all excited," Martha said. "Will you be going to the chapel to pray in the morning like you usually do?"

"Yes, why?"

"Because I'd like to come with you."

Isadora merely shrugged, it was not her business to bother much about other people's issues. "Well, I can't stop you from wasting your sleeping time. You of course know that I usually go there at four."

"Don't worry, for Father John, I'll even wake up at midnight," she grinned.

Martha was the one who woke her up the next morning and as they made their way to the chapel,

Isadora was surprised to find other girls in the chapel and in a short while she understood why.

Father John was not even thirty and he was very handsome. As soon as he entered the chapel at 4.30am, Isadora heard the audible gasps and murmurs which he ignored, instead walking to the altar like Old Father O'Connor used to do. But unlike the old priest who used to concentrate on what he was doing, Father John seemed to be holding a show for his enraptured audience and Isadora felt uncomfortable when she looked around the chapel and saw the girls gazing at the man with adoration in their eyes.

She slipped out when the bell tolled because she didn't want to get in trouble. "Where are you going?" Martha followed her out.

"I have to get to my workplace."

"So what do you think of Father John?" Martha's eyes were glowing. "Isn't he handsome?"

"Martha, pull yourself together. That's a priest you're talking about and if you don't stop all that nonsense, you'll get into trouble."

"Everyone else is excited too."

"Martha, I have to go. If I were you, I'd go back to the dorm to get ready for the day ahead and stop all that nonsense."

9

UNFOLDING DESTINY

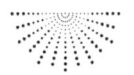

The unexpected news that Rebecca was leaving was received with mixed feelings. There were those girls who cried and said they didn't want her to go but for others like Isadora, the news couldn't have come at a better time.

She was tired of all the abuse she'd taken at the woman's hands and on the day that she finally woke up to hear the Rebecca had found work elsewhere, she rejoiced greatly.

The lady who took her place was called Agatha. She was new to the laundry workhouse and Isadora took an immediate liking to her. She was a quiet woman who took her duties seriously but she was also very kind. Under her guidance, things began to change.

For one, they had enough to eat and the food was much better than they were used to.

And then, Agatha also brought in some carpenters to repair the dormitories and broken beds and for the first time in a long while, the girls had a warm dormitory to go to. Besides that, Isadora was permitted to join her peers for their lessons before the working day began. It was a time of rejoicing for the young woman who had turned seventeen the previous Christmas Day, not that she celebrated it at all. She had stopped celebrating the holiday after her twelfth birthday.

There were times she would sit alone and wonder if Arthur ever thought about her at all. He would now be twenty-two and she imagined him getting engaged to some girl. The thought gave her deep pain.

One morning when she and ten of her friends had finished doing laundry, Marcie came and informed them that the Miss Agatha wanted to see all of them.

"What could we have done wrong?" Jennifer, one of the girls asked. They all looked really scared. Being called by the Matron of the house often meant trouble and possible caning. "Isadora, what did you do that has made us all get into trouble?"

Martha hissed at Jennifer, "Why do you think it's all because of Isadora?"

"Shut up all of you," Marcie stopped and glared at them. "You should all be ashamed of yourselves, pecking at each other like hungry hens. The next person who speaks a word will get a proper caning from me."

But when they got to the Matron's office, it was to receive news that surprised them all.

"Isadora and others," Agatha had a smile on her face and her gaze went around the room, resting on all of them. "You're seventeen years old now and I feel that the time for you to take care of yourselves has come."

The eleven girls looked at each other and Agatha laughed. "I'm starting a program where you girls will get placed in good homes as governesses. This will help secure your futures." The girls looked at each other and then back at the matron as if they were dreaming. "I know it sounds too good to be true but believe me, this is really happening. With the help of a convent in London, we've found families for the eleven of you to go to. Once we see that this program is working, we'll be able to send more girls out each year. This will ensure that none of the girls who come to St. Magdalene's Laundry remains destitute."

One girl raised her hand, "Yes, Naomi?"

"Miss, what if I don't want to become a governess but want to take a vow of chastity and remain as a nun for the rest of my life?"

"Then by all means do that," she smiled, wondering if the girl was jesting. "Serving God fully and giving up your whole life isn't meant for everyone. If anyone doesn't want to become a governess but wants to join the convent who have so graciously helped us, then we'll make enquiries for you to do so. Otherwise, the rest of you should be ready to leave for London in a week's time."

Martha could barely contain herself, "Will we have to come back here ever?"

Agatha shook her head, "Not unless you want to. Otherwise, we're hoping that you will work and eventually meet nice young men and get married and have families. Once you leave St. Magdalene's you don't have to ever return unless it's your personal choice to do so."

10

HOUR OF LIGHT

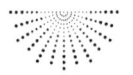

Isadora stared at the massive gates as the carriage drew closer to them. Then as if by magic, they opened by themselves and she gasped when she saw the house at the end of the driveway. It was beautiful and it looked like a place where she could finally be happy.

The two children who ran alongside the carriage as it drew closer to the house were shouting happily and she felt a warm glow within. The last time anyone had been happy to see her was years ago and the thought saddened her a little.

"Isadora," Agatha called out softly. She had made it her personal mission to deliver each girl to the family she was to serve.

"Yes, Miss Agatha?"

"This is going to be your new home. The Wallace family is very kind and if you do your best, they will help you in your life."

"Thank you so much," Isadora's eyes were shining and Agatha sighed inwardly. This child had been through so much and this was a good break for her. A job as a governess in London would change her life story and hopefully bring her the joy that had so long evaded her.

Cara and Bruce Wallace were waiting at the front door and when the carriage stopped, both came down the steps to meet them. "Agatha," they seemed to know her well, "We're so happy to see you," Cara said. "Is this the young lady you wrote to us about?"

"Yes, my dears," she smiled at the two children who were silently observing what was going on. "Her name is Isadora Fontaine and she's one of the best girls at Magdalene's. We've trained them well and apart from just teaching the children, she knows how to paint, crotchet, knit and sew. One of the subjects taught is carpentry even though they are girls. This means that she can build small toys for the children."

Cara smiled at Isadora and then looked toward the carriage. "Will the footman bring her luggage in or should I ask one of the servants to do it?"

Isadora looked down at the small bag at her feet, "Ma'am, this is all my luggage," she said in a soft voice.

Cara and Bruce looked at each other but it was the former who spoke. "We're sorry to keep you standing out here. Would you please come in?"

Agatha shook her head, "I left five other girls at the station. I'd like to return and convey them to their new homes before it gets dark, then I have to return north."

"Thank you so much for bringing Isadora to us," Cara said. "We'll treat her very well."

"I got good references about you from the parish priest and I know that my girl will be happy."

∽

Settling down in the Wallace household was easy because Cara was a good mistress and the children were excited to have a beautiful governess. Bruce Wallace also made her feel comfortable, not like many other men she'd met. He was kind and spent a lot of time in his study working but whenever he emerged, he would concentrate on his children.

In her second week in the household, Isadora got her monthly gift and the pain nearly drove her mad. She was throwing up when Cara came upon her. "Isadora, I hope it's not what I think it is."

"No Ma'am, I'm not with child. It's just that each month when I get my gift from God, it's so painful and lasts two days."

The woman nodded in understanding, "I know just what you mean. It used to be the same way for me but thankfully that's all in the past now."

"What did you take for the pain," Isadora doubled up. "My stomach really hurts."

"I know how terrible it can be. Why don't you take two days off? Mr. Bruce and I were thinking of visiting his mother and this is as good a time as any, and we'll take the children with us."

"I'm really sorry for the inconvenience I'm causing you."

"Isadora," Cara touched her arm, "You have no control over what happens to your body. Just take time to rest and I'll tell the other servants to take good care of you while we're away. We'll be gone for three days and I hope you'll be feeling fine by the time we return."

Left to her own devices, Isadora was able to get much needed sleep. The housekeeper was a woman in her mid-thirties and her name was Lillian Font but everyone called her Lilly. She was kind and for the three days, came up to Isadora's room to keep her company.

"How did you end up at the laundry?" Asked Lilly. "Were you unable to get married and have children of your own? You're really good with the little ones."

"My stepmother made me go there. For many years it was an awful prison, but thank God, Agatha came was so kind to us all. It is because of her that many of us got positions as governesses."

"Well, you're so beautiful and I'm sure a number of young men have told you so."

"There were no young men at the workhouse."

"Are you telling me that you've been in that place all your life?"

Isadora shook her head, "I joined when I was twelve and now I'm seventeen."

"Well, don't worry, Mrs. Cara often gives us time to go to town and meet friends. The next time we're allowed to do so, I'll ask one of the other girls to take you with her. Who knows, you might just meet a fine young man who will steal your heart and then we'll soon be hearing wedding bells."

Isadora joined in Lilly's laughter but knew that she would do no such thing. She couldn't stop thinking about Arthur and wondering what he was doing, what he'd been up to for the past five years. Did he ever think about her?

"From the expression on your face, I have the feeling that your heart belongs to someone."

Her words shocked Isadora to the core because it was true. Her heart belonged to Arthur and she knew that she could never love another man the way she loved him. It took her great effort not to cry out because she realised that her stepmother was right. She was a terrible child who had committed an abomination. How could she be in love with her own half-brother? The thought horrified her, but her heart would not relent.

11
HEALING WATERS

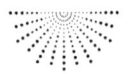

Arthur's meeting with his father's lawyer took place at the lawyer's office. It was neither an easy nor a pleasant session but this had to be done. For five years, he'd put off settling his father's affairs because it all felt so final.

Five years ago, his whole world had fallen apart and it had taken him this long to make sense of it all. No wonder it had taken him this long to settle his father's affairs. And also, as a soon-to-be married man, he needed to know all about the estate.

"Mr. Fontaine, you look really sad."

"This is a really tough for me," Arthur shook his head. "All my life, I thought my father would always been there to take care of things. It never once occurred to me that I would have to settle my father's estate, at least not this soon and certainly not in this way."

"I really understand what you must be going through. Your father was a very meticulous man in his day and his affairs are very much in order. In any case, whatever investments he made were very lucrative in the last five years and you stand to inherit a very large sum."

"All that is worth nothing to me," Arthur cleared his throat. "I would give anything and everything in the world just to have one more minute with my father."

"Losing a parent is never easy but you're now the man of the family and as Edgar's sole heir, everything he owned now belongs to you, except for one issue."

"What's that?"

The lawyer looked slightly uncomfortable, "Do you know a young woman named Isadora?"

Arthur's heart started pounding, "Have you seen her? Do you know where she is?"

"Mr. Fontaine..."

"Please call me Arthur," he said, impatiently waiting for the man to tell him about Isadora. "What about Isadora?"

"No, I haven't seen her, nor do I know where she is. It's just that your father set up a trust fund for her nine years ago after her mother died. According to the terms of the trust, when she turns twenty-one, she will inherit quite a substantial amount of money. With your father dead, I was hoping that you might know where I could find her so that I can do the needful."

Arthur's heart sank, "Isadora lived with us for four years but after Papa died, she ran away. I've been searching for her these five years but so far, I haven't heard as much as a whisper about her."

"Some young women decide to go to America and she might be one of them. Or else Europe too, have you thought about that?"

"She was very innocent and naive and my fear is that someone may have kidnapped her and done something terrible to her."

"Don't always think of the worst case scenario. Tell yourself that wherever she is, the girl is happy and doing well. Otherwise you will trouble your mind with needless anxiety."

"What will happen if Isadora is never found, what will you do with the trust fund?"

"It will be held for ten years from the time she turns twenty-one and then it will revert back to your father's estate so you might well end up getting that too."

"I don't want it, I'd rather that the money goes to charity than to put it back in the estate."

"Since the girl still has another four years before she turns twenty-one, let's not talk of matters that most likely may not happen."

12

THE BRIDGE BUILDER

Isadora and the children ran the last mile to the house, laughing all the way. They arrived to find Cara and Bruce standing on the steps waiting for them.

"Oh Mama," Lauren's little face was lit up, "It was so much fun. Miss Isadora is very nice."

"I can see that you had a wonderful time," Cara smiled at Isadora.

"Papa," Wesley tugged at his father's shirt, "Papa, let me tell you something."

"Yes, my little man?" Bruce crouched to his son's level. "Did something happen when you were out on the trip?"

"Yes, we saw a bird's nest and Miss Isadora told us not to disturb it. But there were eggs inside. I wanted to take one but Miss Isadora said their mama would be sad."

"And she was right, son," Bruce ruffled his son's hair. "When you take little ones away from their Mamas, you destroy a family."

"But Pa, those were just eggs."

"And little ones come out from those eggs. So if you take away even one egg, you're taking away Mrs. Birdie's little child."

"Oh," Wesley put his hands over his lips. "Papa, I will never take away anyone's little child."

~

Isadora was smiling when she put the two children to bed in the nursery. Her bedroom was right next to theirs so she could get to them should they need her in the night but they were good children who slept through the night. She'd never had any trouble with any of them since her arrival.

Cara and Bruce Wallace were also a lovely couple and just by looking at them, she could see how much they loved each other. Bruce was thoughtful and did small things for his wife just because.

The next few days were spent by the children drawing whatever they had seen on their walks outside and Isadora was quite impressed. One afternoon as they were frolicking on the front lawn, Isadora was going through one of the dailies when something caught her eye.

Engagement Notice

Mrs. Clarissa Fontaine, wife of the late Mr. Edgar Fontaine of Oxford Village, is pleased to announce the engagement of her only son Arthur Wilson Fontaine to Miss Margaret Piper, second daughter to Mr. Thomas and Mrs. Anne Piper of Oxford Village.

Isadora couldn't carry on reading the rest of the notice and she didn't realise that she was crying until Cara walked onto the lawn carrying a pitcher of lemonade and some tumblers. "What's wrong, Isadora?" She was whispering so the children wouldn't overhear them. "Why are you crying?" She placed the pitcher and tumblers on the small lawn table then sat down opposite Isadora. "What's making you so sad?"

"Oh Cara," she looked down at the picture and advertisement.

"Who is that?"

"My half-brother," her head was bowed so she didn't see Cara's curious look. "He never once wrote to find out how I was doing at school even though I wrote several letters to him. Now I know the reason why."

"You sound jealous of your brother's engagement."

Isadora turned red because it was true. She was really jealous of the relationship her brother had with Maggie but she had never once thought that he would get engaged to the girl. Well, he was now twenty-three years old and ready to marry and settle down.

"I'm just being silly," she gave a small laugh and folded the paper. "Lauren and Wesley are nearly done playing," she tried to change the subject so Cara wouldn't ask her more questions because she was really confused about her feelings for her half-brother. What was wrong with her? Could her mother be right about her being a terrible person?

"It's normal for siblings to feel jealous of the other person's partner especially if they were very close growing up."

"That's right," she said, trying to smile.

"Don't worry, I'm sure that your brother will one day reach out and find you."

Isadora shook her head, "Were my father still alive, I would have that hope. But after he died, that relationship ended."

13

THE OPEN DOOR

For the rest of his life, Arthur would always remember where he was and what he was doing on the day that his father walked back into the house. He was in his father's study going through the books of accounts. He'd never realised just how wealthy his father was until the lawyer told him. Edgar had owned five large cargo ships aside from the one on which he and his whole crew had perished. As a way of introducing him to his father's assets, the lawyer had made arrangements for him to travel to Liverpool and meet with the man managing the fleet.

Arthur was thinking about his journey and how his mother and fiancée would react to the news of him being away from home for at least two months, when he heard a firm footfall in the hallway. Only one person he knew used to walk that way and Arthur held his head in his hands. Why couldn't he stop thinking about his father? But as the steps drew closer to the study door, he was forced to look up when they stopped and the knob was turned.

To his shock, the person who stood there in the doorway was Edgar himself. He was a

little thinner and had grown a long beard but it was his father, alive and in the flesh. At first, Arthur thought he was seeing a ghost and just sat there, mouth wide open and his face as white as a sheet.

Edgar chuckled softly, the deep sound permeating the whole house. "Son, you look like you've seen a ghost."

"Father?" Arthur slowly rose to his feet. "Papa, am I dreaming or is it really you?"

"Son, come here," Edgar held his arms out and Arthur needed no second bidding. His father was alive and as father and son hugged, they didn't hold back their tears.

"You've grown up in the past five years," Edgar looked over his son's shoulder, "I expected to find Isadora hanging on a tree or on the chimney," he grinned. "Where is she anyway?"

Arthur sighed and moved away from his father, "Papa, Isadora hasn't been home for five years."

"What do you mean?"

"Pa, when you disappeared, we heard that your ship sank and you and the crew all perished. We held a memorial service for you and on the same night, Isadora ran away from home."

"Who told you that she ran away?"

"It was Mama but I'm starting to think that she was right. Isadora didn't like it here and decided to go back to where she'd come from."

"Arthur," Edgar sat down tiredly on the couch, "I brought Isadora to this house when she was eight years old, after her mother had died. She had no relatives and so I don't believe she ran away. Something happened," he looked angry. "Where is your mother?"

"Mama is visiting some friends. She was invited to a soiree but she should be back soon."

"I know the servants want to see me since the footman must have gossiped to them by now. He was the first person to see me when the carriage brought me back."

"Pa, what happened to you?"

Edgar ruffled his grown up son's hair, "I'll tell you everything when your mother returns so I don't have to repeat myself. But just know this, I'm really happy to be home."

"And I'm happy that you're home, Papa."

~

To say that Clarissa was surprised to see her husband was putting it mildly. When she walked into her house and found him in the drawing room with Arthur, she became like one turned to stone.

"Clarissa," Edgar rose to his feet. "It's not a ghost, it's really I."

"Edgar," she rushed forward and hugged him. "Where have you been these five years?"

"I was just about to tell Arthur. Why don't you sit down and I'll tell you everything?"

~

When he'd left the house on Christmas Day after imagining that his children had done something terrible, he couldn't face returning. So he decided to travel to Liverpool to check on his ships which were docked there. His intention was to stay away only two or three days but then when he got there, found that there was a slight problem with one of his ships which had sailed for America.

Rashly, he decided to travel to America and sort the problem out. "We encountered very strong winds which blew us off course and we ended up shipwrecked on a small island. Mercifully, the inhabitants had received missionaries in years past so they welcomed us. We were there for five years but then an epidemic wiped out nearly half the population including my crew," Edgar smiled sadly. "We lost good men but didn't give up. Then a few weeks later, someone spotted a sail. We started a fire and the ship came close enough for us to swim out to it and that's how I was saved and came back home."

14
WEEP NO MORE

"I know that my son made a promise of marriage to your daughter but it had to have been made while he was under duress," Edgar faced the Pipers without flinching. Arthur couldn't believe the change that had come over his father. Previously, he would have allowed the Pipers to walk all over him and make the decision but not now. It was like his father was a new man.

"Our daughter was greatly traumatized when she received your son's note breaking their engagement off," Thomas Piper said, his eyes flashing angrily at Arthur then back to Edgar. "What kind of a man proposes to a woman and then changes his mind at the last minute?"

"Thomas, I'm very sorry for all that happened in my absence for the past five years. You all know that I wasn't here to guide my son's ways because of what happened to me," Edgar said firmly. "He's a good boy and I know that when he gave in to the engagement, it was because he was not properly advised. Once again, Mr. and Mrs. Piper, please convey our humblest and deepest apologies to Miss Margaret. It wasn't Arthur's intention to hurt her but he can't marry her when he's not prepared to do so."

"I'll broadcast this ill against our daughter to everyone and we shall see if any other good family will allow him to court their daughter. This is deeply embarrassing and I don't know what we're going to do," Thomas looked at his wife who sat there with a white face. "The shame of people talking about our Maggie is too much."

"Perhaps sir, I can be of help."

"What more do you want to do? Edgar, your son has broken our daughter's heart and she is inconsolable."

"Which is the reason why I would like to offer her the chance to go on a trip to Paris or Cannes, whichever she desires with hopes that her spirits will be lifted and if possible, restored once again."

Those words brought back the colour into Anne Piper's face and Arthur smiled inwardly at his father's shrewdness. He was using Anne's love for the good life to solve the problem that was lying before them.

"If you agree, Thomas, I'll immediately make arrangements for the young lady and her mother to be gone for three months. They will find that visiting France at this time will be very productive for them. Many good families I know of are also visiting on holiday and who knows, the young lady may just find a better man than my son."

"Oh Thomas," Anne's eyes were glowing, "This is just what might make our Maggie come to life again."

Thomas didn't look as easily convinced as his wife. "What will you do in Paris or Cannes?" He asked roughly.

"Sir, if I may," Edgar cleared his throat, "The money that might have been spent on the wedding is lying unused, and it's the sum of five thousand pounds. What if I was to gift that to the young woman as a way of saying sorry, something like a consolation prize; would that be of any help?"

That brought a reluctant smile to the irate man's lips. "If her mother and the girl are willing then I see no problem."

"I'm very sorry about all this," Arthur said in a soft voice.

"Don't worry son," Thomas looked mellow, "These things happen and the time away will do our Maggie good."

"May I just see her to tell her how sorry I am?"

Edgar and Thomas both shook their heads but it was the former who spoke. "Son, I don't think it's the right thing to do. Miss Margaret's parents will take care of her and convey your apologies. We need to be going now, your mother will be worrying."

Which wasn't true because Arthur remembered how angry his mother had been when his father supported him in his desire to end the engagement that was weighing down on him. They had left her back at the house really fuming but his father had overruled any protests she might have had.

The moment they were clear of the house, Arthur turned to his father, "Papa, I'm very sorry for putting you in that situation."

"Don't you worry a thing about it. I just hope that you won't get to a point where you'll regret breaking off the engagement. Margaret Piper is a good young woman from a respectable family. You could have done worse."

"Papa, I thought I could go through with it at the time but now," he shook his head, "Margaret Piper isn't the woman that my heart wants and it would be grossly unfair for me to marry her while knowing full well that I can never love her the way she deserves to be loved and cherished. You always told me to be true to myself and to others and at the time of accepting to be engaged to Maggie, I was overwhelmed by all that had happened first with you gone missing and presumed dead and then Isadora running away from home. It was easier just to give in to Mama's pressure."

"Then I'm glad that I came back when I did."

15

A MATTER OF TIME

There was a knock at her door and Isadora looked up from the small desk where she'd been doodling with her finger. The children were downstairs with their parents and they never knocked so she guessed that it might be one of the servants. "Come in." The door opened and Cara stepped into the room, a slight frown on her brow.

"Isadora, the children tell me that once again, you don't want to celebrate Christmas with us."

Isadora shook her head, "Please, I'm sorry to be trouble to you."

"No, you don't have to apologize for that. I understand that not everyone goes overboard with the holidays at this time of year but we would like for you to at least join us for the midday meal."

"If you don't mind, may I be excused?"

"Is there a good reason for this? Last year, you didn't want to celebrate with us and we thought you were ill. But two years in a row means something else."

Isadora sighed, "It's just that from when I was twelve, Christmas became a time of pain and sorrow for me and I don't see the need to celebrate it. All I see when the holiday comes around is pain and anguish and I just wish I could go to sleep in November and wake up in January when it's all over."

"It must have been something so terrible."

"My father left home on Christmas Day eight years ago and one week later, we got the news that his ship had sunk and with him and the whole crew on board." She bowed her head and let the tears flow. "My father died around the Christmas season," Isadora felt so much shame about her role in all that. But it wasn't something she was willing to divulge to her mistress. "I can never celebrate Christmas again, knowing what I lost at the time. And then I was sent off to the workhouse by my stepmother who didn't want me. So you can understand why I don't find anything good to celebrate at this time."

16

UP IN FLAMES

The terror which would not end for another full year began with a strange carriage standing in the driveway. Spring was in the air and the weather was too good for her to keep the children indoors and when she suggested a walk, they jumped at the chance. It had been a long and cold winter and the sunshine was welcome.

Like she did every day since coming to work for the Wallace family, Isadora had taken Lauren and Wesley out on one of their famous nature walks. The children enjoyed the outdoors, and so did she, especially after the five years of being locked up and mostly in isolation back at the workhouse laundry. Any chance she got, she would spend it outside and had even arranged for the children to have some of their lessons out in the open air.

They returned to the house just a few minutes before noon so the children could wash up and get ready for their lunch. The moment Isadora saw the strange carriage, something within deflated even before she saw who the occupants were.

"Visitors," Lauren shouted and ran toward the back of the house, her brother hot in pursuit. The Wallace children were very well behaved in that they never used the front door when their parents had visitors.

Something about the carriage frightened Isadora and the moment she walked into the house and heard the visitor's voice, she knew the end of her joy had come.

"Isadora," Lilly the housekeeper called out to her as she crossed through the kitchen. "Mrs. Wallace said you should go up to your room, pack your bags and leave at once."

"Why? What did I do?"

"It's not for you to ask questions and me to answer them. Mr. and Mrs. Wallace don't want to see you in their home again."

"I understand," Isadora said, quite defeated. She was sure that her old nemesis, Rebecca, had told lies about her and caused the previously kind people to turn against her.

She was waiting at the carriage when Rebecca came out of the house. Cara and Bruce didn't even come to the door and she knew that the ex-workhouse matron had told them only the worst about her. She didn't blame them at all, even though she could hear the children screaming in the house. Their parents were probably telling them that Isadora had to leave and they were having none of that.

"Get in," were the only words all Rebecca said all the way to the train station and then on the trip back north. The moment the workhouse gates clanged shut behind her, Isadora knew that she would never leave this place again.

Rebecca had returned at the behest of the workhouse laundry owners. Agatha it seems did not encourage the girls and women to work hard enough, and the loss of good labor to other employment was hurting their bottom line.

17
ABYSS OF THOUGHT

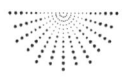

Somewhere below the chapel, the drain was quickly filling up with mud faster than Isadora could empty it. This was another of the punishments that had been meted out to her and she was feeling very frustrated with everything that was going on.

It was like Rebecca was out to destroy her life and break her spirit completely. And she was succeeding because Isadora felt like there was no more hope for her. She had returned to the laundry wondering if the Wallace's had withheld all her wages for the two years that she'd worked for them.

But then Rebecca gleefully shattered her world again. "Since you're destined to be here for the rest of your life, you won't need the money. The

Wallace's gave me all the money you made working for them for these past two years," the woman had actually smiled at her. "They were paying you good money and it's going to really help out here."

"Why did you have them terminate my services? I really wanted to work for them because Miss Agatha said it would be a chance for me to prepare for my future."

"Well, Miss Agatha was wrong. Besides, once they found out that you had lain with your brother, they wanted nothing more to do with you because you were a bad influence on the children. No parent wants to hire a woman who was in an incestuous relationship and caused problems in the family."

Once again, the joy had been snatched from her and all that was left was despair. If she didn't fear so much, she would probably have ended her life months ago. It was like life was out to get her and show her who the master was.

"Isadora, are you almost finished?" Mary Ruben's voice floated from somewhere above her. "Miss Rebecca told me to come and check on you." Mary had taken Martha's place in Isadora's life. Of the other girls who'd left the workhouse laundry with her, none of them had returned. But sadly, Agatha was let go and Isadora knew that there was no one else to support or defend her from the now returned Rebecca.

"I'm almost done," she answered.

"Do you need any help?"

"I don't want you to get all muddied up like I am."

But Mary came down anyway and then sighed with dismay when she saw the mess. "Oh dear," she looked down at the drain. "You'll never get this done, at least not this year."

"If only the rain would cease even for a few minutes, I would be able to get all this cleaned up."

18

EDGE OF THE SWORD

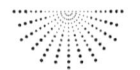

Isadora stared at Father John and chewed her lip nervously. As always, she'd come to the chapel early in the morning to pray and expected to find his usual band of admirers with him but the place was empty. As she sat down in a pew and got ready to pray, she heard footsteps and then he came and stood beside her. He frightened her but she didn't want to show him that she was vulnerable. She'd been glad to leave this place and but now here she was, back in the place of her nightmares.

"Good morning, child, what's your name?"

"Isadora Fontaine," she said, in a trembling voice. Father O'Connor had treated her kindly and she sincerely hoped that his younger replacement would follow in his footsteps. Her fear of men continued to hound her with fears of molestation and abuse, even when no reason to fear presented itself.

"That's a very pretty name," he said and she frowned. Should a priest be saying such things to her? "But the name is not as pretty as the person who bears it."

Isadora crossed herself, bowed her head and pretended to be praying, hoping he would walk away. Her heart was pounding in her chest because she had never expected a priest to speak to her like this. She sighed in relief when the priest walked away, and then there were footsteps of people entering the chapel.

She couldn't shake off the feeling that this man was what Reverend George Simms had called a wolf in sheepskin. The vicar, during one of his sermons, had talked about those who came as angels of light and yet all they carried within them was darkness. She wondered if she should share her fears with anyone, or were they just monsters dredged up from her imagination.

For the next few days, Isadora avoided going to the chapel very early because she didn't want to run into the priest. But one morning, she woke up very early and as usual, walked to the chapel. It was empty and just as she was about to turn and leave, she felt a presence behind her.

She was about to turn around but strong hands grasped her and prevented her. A man was blocking her path.

"Father John?"

"Isadora."

The voice was not that of father John.

"Isadora, it has been a long time."

Isadora instantly recognised the voice of Peter, Rebecca's nephew. Isadora thought that he had left when his aunt had, but now it appears he returned with her too.

"Have you missed me?' Peter's voice sounded like the serpent in the garden.

"No, sir," she said, trying to sidestep and escape but he blocked her path. "Please."

"You're a beautiful girl and I've no doubt that many men have told you that already when you were outside these walls," he reached out a hand and cupped her chin. "Why are you pretending that you don't like me when I can see it in your eyes? Or are you hoping that by acting coyly you'll get my attention?" He smiled and it reminded her of a wolf baring its fangs. "Well, you have my attention now, sweet Isadora."

She pulled her chin away and stepped backwards.

"We shouldn't let such an opportunity go by, should we?" He growled, drawing closer. She retreated until her back was against the wall and then realised her mistake. He bore down and pinned her to the wall and she started struggling, really afraid that he was losing control. "Just one kiss from your sweet lips is all I ask for," he said, clearly losing control and Isadora opened her mouth to scream but he quickly covered it with his lips. She struggled to get free but he was stronger than her and she prayed that someone would come so she could get away from him.

"What are you doing?" Father John's harsh voice caused Peter to jump back. He collapsed against the wall and started sobbing. "What is going on here, Peter?"

"This evil seductress came at me," he pointed at Isadora who stood like one frozen. Her clothes were all dishevelled. "She begged me to take her out of here and promised me her favours."

"That's not true," Isadora shouted. "I came here to pray and you pounced on me."

Father John drew closer and pushed Peter against the wall.

"Do you realise that you're dealing with a servant of God?" Father John asked the trembling man in his hands. "How dare you touch any one of these girls."

"But, but…" Peter protested weakly.

"Sir, you will be openly shamed if I hear of one more transgression. Now go!"

Peter ran from the chapel.

"Dear Isadora, are you alright, my dear?"

"Yes, sir. I think so."

"Go back to your dormitory. I will speak to the matron about this sorry event, and ensure that Peter does not harass you again."

~

Rebecca slapped Isadora.

"I knew you were trouble but didn't think you were shameless enough to try and lure a good man into sin." After another resounding slap, Rebecca grabbed

Isadora by the collar and dragged her all the way to the courtyard.

"This is an evil girl and should be punished," she screamed at the other girls who were present. "Strip her for she needs the demons whipped out of her. She was found trying to seduce Peter."

Isadora's cries could be heard throughout the building as the whip cruelly tore her back.

19

NOTHING IN THE DREAMS

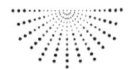

As Christmas season approached, Arthur told his father that it was the worst one ever. Two years and many months of searching for Isadora had proved futile. She wasn't in London where they knew most runaways headed to. Neither was she in Manchester, Liverpool or any of the other cities where they had people searching for her.

Money was not a problem in as far as Edgar was concerned and he hired as many detectives as he could to try and find her.

"Christmas will never be the same again for me, Pa," Arthur sat with his head bowed. He'd just found the painting of the bird that Isadora had drawn for him so many years before and it caused tears to flow down his cheeks. He missed her more than ever and he didn't know how he was going to face the days ahead. While they were still searching for her, he'd been hopeful that she would be found and they would be reconciled. But hope seemed to be fading away and he knew that they couldn't go on searching for the rest of their lives. They were going to have to stop at some point and the thought caused him anguish.

"I know you miss Isadora, we all do but we can't give up hope."

"Where could she be?"

Edgar shook his head, "Son, I wish I knew for then I would immediately go there and bring her back home."

"Pa?"

"Yes, son?"

"There's something I have to tell you," Arthur bit his bottom lip. "I did something terrible."

Edgar frowned slightly and came closer to his son. "What do you mean?"

"It's all my fault that Isadora ran away."

"I don't think so but what makes you feel that way?"

Arthur turned a bright red, "Pa, I was seventeen when Isadora left home. For a long time, I'd been feeling funny around her and I know it wasn't right."

"I don't understand what you're saying, Arthur."

"Pa, I was attracted to my sister," he looked down. "That day when Isadora fell asleep on my bed, I wanted to kiss her but not like a sister. I should never have let her remain there. I did not do it, but I was so ashamed of my feelings I failed to speak up for her."

Edgar gave his son a curious look. "Do you realise what you're telling me?"

The young man nodded, "Yes, Father. I am the sinful one and what's worse, it's Isadora who is paying for my sins."

20

THE HEALING PETALS OF CHRISTMAS

They strolled along the corridor in the house holding hands and grinning like fools. Edgar was somewhere in the house and they could hear the servants chattering happily. The house seemed to have come alive. "I never believed that I could ever be this happy," Isadora wanted to pinch herself to make sure she wasn't sleeping.

"Isadora," Arthur said her name in a way that sent delightful shivers run down her back. This was her husband, the man she'd been in love with for so long and who she'd thought she would never see again. He was here, he was holding her hand and he'd just placed a beautiful wedding ring on her finger. "Isadora," he repeated.

"I'm right here," she whispered.

"I thought I had lost you forever," he stopped and turned her so they were facing each other. "For eight years, you were gone from my life and I never thought I'd ever see you again."

It all seemed like a dream to both of them. Several days after Isadora had been rescued from the laundry workhouse, she'd runaway and ended up at the vicar's house. After eight hours of weeping and confessing and being comforted, she was finally ready to forgive all those who had hurt her.

When the vicar and his wife walked her home, they found the whole household in an uproar. The moment Arthur saw her, he ran and took her in his arms but was mindful of her injured back.

"Isadora," he'd cried with tears in his eyes and she gave him a watery smile of her own.

"Here I am." She whispered.

The three of them sat down to talk and it was hours before they went to bed to rest, but not before Arthur asked Edgar for his permission to marry Isadora. He'd given his consent and even requested the vicar to obtain a special license for them to get married.

"What are you thinking about?" Arthur's voice broke into her thoughts. "Isadora, my love, I don't want you to ever be sad again."

"I know that I can't predict the future but I have a feeling that the worst is behind us all."

"You're a very brave woman, Isadora."

"Arthur, this isn't the time for tears," she allowed him to hold her close. "Let's try and put the past behind us and live for the future."

"I'd like that very much."

They had walked to living room where a fire was burning merrily in the grate. "This house is so full of laughter."

"And that's the way it will be forever," Arthur promised. "We'll do our best to help those who need it."

"I just feel sad for the girls I left in the workhouse. With all that happened, Rebecca might really take it out on them."

But Arthur was shaking his head. "Papa sent his lawyer there and we got the report that after we left, that fierce looking constable hauled Rebecca away. Sister Angelica, the dear lady of God who was kind to you is now overseeing St Magdalene's. You can be sure that the wicked woman who caused you so much pain will never again do so to anyone else."

"But what about Peter, was he taken by the policeman also?"

Arthur shook his head, not sure how Isadora would take the news. "He was found hanging in his room. Apparently, he knew that his actions would be exposed and he chose to end his own life."

"What a terrible way to go."

"It's really sad but I don't want us to dwell on the pain. Let's talk about something else."

"With much pleasure," Isadora sank down on the couch and her husband took his place beside her.

"Do you know that I love you so much, Isadora?"

"Not more than I love you," she grinned at him. "Did you ever think that this day would come?" She asked in a soft voice.

"I prayed and hoped," he said. "Deep down I knew that we were meant to be together but then it tore me apart when I thought that we were brother and sister. My mother knew the truth all along but hid it from us so she could torment us."

"Arthur," Isadora reached out a hand and touched his cheek. "We have every right to be angry at Mrs. Clarissa but let's choose to forgive and put that behind us. She paid for her sins and we shouldn't hold on to the past mistakes. From here and now, let's just take this as our God ordained journey and move forward."

"You're a very sweet girl," he kissed her on the lips. "This was indeed a Christmas to remember."

"As it is for me," she smiled. "I woke up in the workhouse on Christmas Day, having lost all hope but by evening, a great miracle had happened and I was back home."

"Christmas celebrates the birth of our Saviour, but I do believe that this year it was also a day of resurrection and return! You have been returned to me, and a new life awaits us. The old is gone, the new has come!"

"Arthur, are we dreaming?"

Arthur merely sighed and pulled his wife close. Not only had he found Isadora, the love of his life, but she was now his wife. And he would cherish her and keep her safe for as long as he lived, that was the promise he made in his heart. That night they ushered in a brand new year, the first of many happy years to come.

21
TROUBLED THOUGHTS

Edgar kept his peace until the twentieth day of December which was just five days to Christmas and dear lost Isadora's birthday. Then he confronted his wife because he needed answers about the whereabouts of his missing daughter.

"For the last time, Clarissa, you will tell me why Isadora left home. And none of that nonsense you've perpetrated about her being a disturbed child. She was just a growing girl trying to find her way but you couldn't see that because you were so bent on getting rid of her."

Clarissa simply pouted and tried to outstare her husband like she'd done in the past. But this time she realised that things had changed. Edgar didn't fidget or hastily look away as he would previously have done. Instead, his dark eyes stared intently at her and she was the first one to look away. He wasn't the same man she'd henpecked for years and she felt fear in her heart.

"Well, seeing as you've refused to talk to me, I'm going to take matters into my own hands."

"What do you mean by that," she asked fearfully.

"Don't worry," he gave her a tight smile, "You'll know soon enough."

"Edgar please."

"What?"

"You were gone for five years and everyone thought you were dead. You've been back for over two years but we seem to be drifting apart instead of getting closer. I missed you," she moved closer and tried to put her arms around him but he sidestepped her.

"Bring me back my daughter and then we can talk about getting closer," and so saying, he left the room. He returned and wagged a finger at her, "Just know this, my good wife, your evil deeds and sins will soon find you out."

Arthur had been eavesdropping on his parents' conversation and wanted to enter the room and defend his mother. Maybe as she said, Isadora had really run away from home. How many times in the past had she threatened to do so, but he would find her and stop her? What if his mother was really telling the truth and Isadora had finally managed to run away?

But would she have done it without telling him? He nodded slowly, knowing that their relationship had been very strained after Christmas Day eight years ago.

"I really wish I knew what happened," he muttered as he walked back to his bedchamber. Would they ever discover the truth or was Isadora gone forever?

22
HIDDEN DANGER

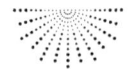

Isadora's love for Arthur wasn't the kind that made girls giggle foolishly, she simply lived with his face in her heart all the time.

For eight years his sweet smile and gentle blue eyes were her repose whenever things got bad. But even with those feelings came deep guilt. She was wicked and would die and end up in hell because she was in love with her own brother. Even though their mothers were different, he was still her father's son and it was wrong in every way for her to have such feelings for him.

Her stepmother and Rebecca were right. She had committed an unpardonable sin and that was the reason why she accepted all her punishment without complaining. She deserved to suffer because of her base feelings.

Christmas Day was approaching and like the past seven, it would most certainly be a sad one for her. While her friends seemed excited at the coming holiday, her own heart was weary because the day was a stark reminder of what she had done and how her deeds had torn her family apart.

"Don't look so gloomy," one of the cooks told her. "Here, why don't you take this pie to eat and cheer your heart."

"Thank you," she smiled at the generous offer. "I'll go and share it with my friends."

The next few days were the most peaceful time Isadora had experienced since she'd come to St. Magdalene's. The temperature warmed and the snow melted and the girls were allowed some free time to make Christmas presents for each other. They had nothing but that didn't stop them from looking for small things to wrap up and exchange.

Isadora reached under her coat and touched the strand of stones around her neck. Years ago, she'd turned the bracelet Arthur gave her into a necklace so it would be out of sight from curious eyes. She had strung the stones together and even though there were only just a few of them, touching the necklace always reminded her of a time when she had really been happy.

What was Arthur doing this Christmas? He was probably married to Maggie Piper and maybe they had a child on the way. She wouldn't cry even though just thinking about it hurt so terribly. Did he ever think of her the way she did of him?

"Isadora, what will you give me for Christmas?" one of her dorm mates asked.

"I need to find some string," she answered her, "then I'll make you a simple necklace."

She decided then and there that she would use the stones from her necklace to make gifts for her friends. In that way, she would get rid of the one thing that was a constant reminder of what she had lost. Yes, the necklace had served its purpose and she hoped that it would bring joy to the other girls.

23

THE BROKEN ROSE

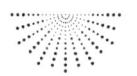

Tears rolled down Isadora's face, stinging her cheeks in the cold night air. When she had lived with Cara and Bruce Wallace she had seen the kind of love they shared, which was so pure and deep. Cara's words came to her again and again, *"Isadora, keep yourself pure for a good man. Let the first kiss you receive be from the lips of a man who loves you and would give his life to protect you. In as much as it depends on you, never allow yourself to be seduced by a man who will only break your heart and leave you despising yourself."*

What kind of a woman was she turning out to be? Just days back, she'd been whipped and humiliated in front of her peers because of Peter's lustful advances, yet she found her mind harassed with thoughts that she was the one who provoked his shameless hunger. Maybe after all she was her indeed her mother's daughter. Harlotry was in her blood.

"Mercy please," she whispered over and over again as she hurried out of the chapel. "Mercy upon my demented soul."

24

THE STRIPPED TWILIGHT

What are you doing?" Clarissa stepped onto the landing and looked down where the servants were busy carrying sacks to the hallway. "What is going on down there?"

It was just two days until Christmas and Arthur was still feeling very sad. Though the servants had decorated the house with holly and boughs as well as bright red, white and green ribbons, it just wasn't the same as when he and Isadora had done it years ago. Christmas would never be the same again, not as long as she was still missing.

"Arthur," his mother's sharp voice brought him out of his thoughts and he shook his head, looking up at her. "I asked you what you're doing. Why are the servants bringing all those sacks to the hallway?"

Arthur merely shrugged, and his father moved into Clarissa's view. "In two days' time, it will be Christmas Day and also Isadora's birthday."

"Your stating of the obvious is rather tiresome, Edgar."

"Well, tiresome or not, we're going to honour Isadora's birthday and donate food, clothes and a sizeable amount of money to the destitute."

Clarissa threw her head back and laughed scornfully, "Oh! So now you want to play the benevolent merchant and his son? Pray tell me, who is going to be the recipient of your half-brained charitable attempts?"

"St. Magdalene's Laundry which is only twenty miles from here," Edgar was bending down and missed seeing the stricken look on his wife's face which had turned as white as a sheet. "It's the nearest workhouse laundry to us and I know those poor orphans will be happy to receive Christmas treats from us. I just wish Isadora was here with us."

Arthur heard his mother's loud gasp and quickly looked up at her standing there on the landing next to the staircase. She swayed and he got concerned.

"Ma, are you alright?"

Clarissa raised the hand that had been holding the balustrade and put it to her forehead like someone who was having a sudden headache. "I ...." and whatever else she was about to say was drowned by her high pitched scream when she missed her footing, tripped over her long robe and came hurtling down the stairs, landing on the floor with a sickening crack and thud.

Father and son as well as the two female servants who were in the hallway stood frozen in shock for a moment before Edgar moved and rushed to his wife's side. Her eyes were closed and she seemed to have lost consciousness. "Quick, Arthur, get one of the male servants to come and help carry your mother up to her bedroom," but apparently they had heard the scream and rushed into the hallway before any call was necessary. Three of them carried the injured woman up to her bedchamber and placed her gently on the bed at Edgar's instructions. Arthur hovered in the doorway, wringing his hands and feeling very helpless.

The doctor arrived nearly an hour later and after thoroughly examining Clarissa, he didn't have good news for them. "Mr. Fontaine, I'm afraid that things are really quite bad for your wife.'

"What's wrong, Doctor?"

"The fall badly affected her back and she's unable to move any other part of her body save for her neck and head. Of course, it could be a temporary thing but she says she's in a lot of pain. I've given her some laudanum for the pain but that is only a temporary solution."

"Doctor, what else can we do to help?"

Dr. Kildare shook his head, "Nothing much for now, I'm afraid. Let's hope the pain subsides. I need to make a few other house calls but I'll be back in the evening to check on Mrs. Fontaine."

"Thank you, doctor."

Arthur could hear his mother groaning in pain and he was really frightened. He had heard the dreadful snap as she fell but even as the doctor tried to lighten things up, he could feel that something was terribly wrong. What if his mother was dying but the doctor didn't want to tell them the truth?

"Arthur," he heard her calling out in a weak voice and he entered the bedchamber.

"Yes, Mama, I'm here."

"Where is your father?" She turned her head to look at him, "Please call him."

"Yes Ma," and he turned to go and get his father but Edgar stepped into the room just then. He walked over to the bed and looked down at his wife.

"Clarissa, don't overtire yourself now. You need to rest."

"Please," she looked at him beseechingly, "Send for the vicar, I need him to pray for me." She looked scared and Arthur felt the tears well up in his eyes. His mother was a proud and strong woman and seeing her lying there helplessly crushed him. "You need to hurry."

"Arthur," his father looked at him.

"I'll leave right now, Pa," he rushed out of the room because he needed to get away. There was an oppressive heaviness in his mother's bedchamber and as he took one of the horses to ride out to the vicar's place, he was praying that it wouldn't be too late.

Reverend Simms silently listened to the weeping woman as she poured her heart out to him but said nothing.

"Why aren't you saying anything?"

"Because, my dear, this confession you're making isn't for me. You need to tell your husband and your son what you just shared with me."

"I can't do that," tears were rolling down the sides of her head. "I don't want them to know what I did."

"Mrs. Fontaine, the only way you can get peace in your heart after what you did is by telling the truth. True, your husband may get angry but he'll eventually forgive you. Edgar is a good man and I know that by making your confession, you will feel better."

"What if he hates me after this? And Arthur, I don't want my son to think badly of me."

"Mrs. Fontaine, we can sit here arguing back and forth the whole day but I believe that deep down in your heart, you know what you need to do."

"I can't do it," she whispered and the vicar rose to his feet. "Where are you going?" Her stricken voice stopped him. "You haven't prayed for me."

He gave her a gentle smile, "Child, of what use is praying for you if you won't acknowledge your wrong doings and ask for forgiveness from the people you hurt most? I can pray yes, but believe me, you won't get any peace."

Clarissa sobbed for a while before she nodded, "Please ask Edgar and Arthur to come in."

"You'll find peace after this, I promise you."

Edgar and Arthur entered the room not knowing what to expect. Arthur sat on the bed and held his mother's hand even though he knew she couldn't feel a thing while Edgar leaned against the wall.

"Mrs. Fontaine asked you to come in because there's something she needs to share with you," the vicar nodded at her and she cleared her throat.

"Please forgive me," she begged, "I wronged you all very much and I want to ask for your forgiveness."

"Ma, please don't overexert yourself because Dr. Kildare said you shouldn't be agitated by anything. You can tell us whatever it is when you're feeling better."

But Clarissa shook her head, "No, it may be too late then," she sobbed. "I was the one who took Isadora away from home eight years ago."

"What?" Arthur dropped her hand and raised his eyes to his father, who didn't look at all surprised by the announcement. "Mother, you told everyone that Isadora had run away from home."

"I lied, please forgive me," since she couldn't move her hands, her eyes did the beseeching for her. "Ever since Isadora came to this house, I had been searching for a way to get rid of her but Edgar wouldn't let me. I looked around for boarding schools and wanted to ask your father to send her to one of them but that was a very sore topic between us. After Edgar's disappearance, I sent for someone to come take her away."

"Who? Where?" Edgar tried to speak as mildly as he could but he was angry. For eight years, Isadora had suffered while his wife kept silent.

"Today when you told me that you were going to take some items to St. Magdalene's, I got frightened because that's where I sent Isadora."

"What?" Father and son looked at each other and then back at Clarissa. It was Edgar's harsh voice which made her wince. "You mean all this time,

Isadora has only been about twenty miles from here?"

"I'm sorry," Clarissa's tears fell thick and heavy. "I paid the matron there, Rebecca, some money and have been doing so every month so she would make sure that Isadora doesn't ever leave the house. Two years ago, Rebecca found work elsewhere, and Isadora was released to work for a family in London as a governess but I knew that I had to get her back or my secret would be made known. Agatha, the new matron, wouldn't tell me where she was but when Rebecca returned, she went and brought Isadora back to the workhouse."

"So even after all you did and the child got some peace, you still followed her to continue hurting her?" Edgar forgot that his wife was lying injured. "What kind of a woman are you?"

"Please forgive me," she sobbed weakly. "Reverend Simms, please pray for me now."

But the vicar shook his head. "You haven't told your family everything, Mrs. Fontaine. They deserve to know the truth, and especially your son."

But Clarissa turned her head away and after a moment, her sobs died down and she made a sound like the whistling of a kettle. "Please forgive me."

"Mrs. Fontaine, we'll let you rest for now."

She turned her head and looked at them, deep sorrow in her eyes. "If you ever find Isadora, please ask her to forgive me."

"We'll leave for Magdelene's right away and bring her back so you can tell her yourself," Edgar said but his wife shook her head.

"It may be too late by then," she turned her eyes to the vicar. "Please absolve me of my sins."

"In a moment, child, but isn't there something else you need to tell your husband and son?"

Clarissa nodded, "Edgar, please forgive me for I sinned against you."

"Is this about Isadora?"

"No," she whispered hoarsely. "At the time we got married ..." her voice trailed off and she turned her head to face the wall.

"Clarissa, if there's something you need to get off your chest then this is the time to do so," Edgar's tone was mild. "You need to rest and we can come back later."

"No," she turned and faced him again. "Arthur is not your son," she announced. "When we got married, I was already with child but I was desperate and didn't know what else to do."

Father and son looked at each other, shock written all over their faces and then back at Clarissa. She closed her eyes and the vicar knew that she wasn't going to be able to tell them anything more.

"Mother, open your eyes and tell me everything," Arthur burst out. He couldn't believe what he was hearing. "Who is my father and why did you do this to me?" He felt like all breath was being squeezed out of him. "Who is my father?"

But Clarissa didn't say a word more and an hour later, she breathed her last.

∽

"About twenty-five years ago, something happened in this parish," Reverend Simms told the two men who looked really stricken. "Edgar, if you can recall, there was that tragedy of the man who lost his wife and two children under mysterious circumstances. He was a middle-aged man named Cuthbert Wiles, and a wealthy trader. Clarissa was his governess but he got so besotted with her that he poisoned his wife and children just to get rid of them so he could be with her."

Arthur didn't want to hear any more but he couldn't get to his feet and walk away. All his life, he'd known his mother was a difficult person but finding out that she was the one who had gotten rid of Isadora was too much, and then hearing her confession that Edgar was not his father.

"Cuthbert came and confessed to me just months after his family's deaths and the guilt was eating at him and he was seriously ill. As he lay on his deathbed, he told me everything, leaving nothing out." The vicar looked at Arthur with much compassion in his eyes, "Cuthbert Wiles was your father, Arthur."

The shame of knowing that he had lived in this household and enjoyed all the benefits when he didn't belong, yet Isadora who was the rightful heiress had suffered and been taken away from home was too much and he broke down.

"I have to leave," he told his father amid the sobs. "I don't belong here. Isadora is the rightful heiress but she was sent away while I took her place."

"Son, listen to me," Edgar's voice was as firm as the hand he placed on Arthur's shoulder. "You are my son and I don't care what anyone else wants to say."

"How can you say that?"

"Because it's true; regardless of what your mother did, you're my son and have always been. From the moment you were born and I held you in my arms, you were mine and nothing will ever change that."

"But what about Isadora?"

"Now that we know where she is, we'll bring her back home on Christmas Day. We would have gone sooner but you know that we have a funeral to plan and tomorrow after we bury your mother, we'll prepare to go and bring Isadora home."

"Can't we go now?"

Edgar shook his head, "You've seen that there are many people coming and going and I need you by my side," Arthur looked up and saw that his father seemed to have aged in a short time. "I'm not as strong as I used to be."

"Yes Father, I'll be by your side."

"And there's something else," Edgar smiled at him. "Isadora's mother told me that she was my child but I knew it couldn't be true, nevertheless, I loved that child from the moment I saw her twenty years ago, on Christmas Day." He shook his head. "I was young and foolish and Rita Bowers was like a drug that I couldn't get out of my system. But on that day, I had decided that I was going to end the affair because I had made a promise to you and your mother that things were going to change. However, when I got to her house, I found out that she'd given birth to a little girl. Something in my heart wanted the child to be mine and when I asked Rita about it and she said Isadora was my daughter, I accepted it. But deep down, I knew that she was lying about that just as she lied about nearly everything else, yet I couldn't turn my back on Isadora. That's why I brought her here after her mother died."

Arthur didn't know whether to laugh or cry. He felt like a heavy weight had been lifted off his shoulders. He and Isadora weren't related by blood, she wasn't his half-sister and he found himself smiling.

"Why are you smiling?"

"Nothing," he told his father. "I just thought of something that has made me smile, that's all."

25

HOUR OF DARKNESS

"I would rather die than give in to you," Isadora hissed. She had come into the chapel much earlier than her normal because Rebecca had told her to clear the place of cobwebs. The ceiling was quite high and she had brought a long stick to try and get rid of as many of the cobwebs as she could, which was proving quite futile. She would have to find a way of climbing up so she could do a better job. But just as she was thinking about that, Peter had walked in.

∼

"I'm filled with loathing and disgust when I think of my life. I may be the daughter of a fallen woman, but I refuse to follow such ways. Let me be and go from here, Peter, before Father John finds you again and broadcasts your shame to the parish."

"Do you think you're the first girl to resist me?" He mocked her. "Your so-called friends are always throwing themselves at me, do you think you're so special?"

Isadora thought for a moment and then smiled. Yes, Cara had told her that she was special and as such, should always maintain her dignity. *"When you value yourself, others will do so too. But if you treat yourself like you're some cheap thing, then you will make others treat you in the same way, Isadora. Remember this if nothing else, we teach people how to treat us."*

She raised her face up to Peter with resolve, "Yes, Peter, I know that I'm a special person and that is why I'll never allow you or anyone else to disrespect or dishonour me. Now, would you please leave so I can finish removing cobwebs from the ceiling?"

"You're a delinquent and an insolent girl," Peter told her but he stood at a safe distance from her, his eyes darting from her face to the large stick she held in her hands. "I'll tell Rebecca that you've been rude to me and you will really get it."

"Good," Isadora retorted back.

"You're an incestuous sinner and your deranged soul will burn in eternal hell. Your sins can never be absolved because you're still an undisciplined and disobedient woman."

"You're also an evil man for what you've done to innocent girls here," Isadora was tired of being silent. "I may be going to hell and after I get there, but as sure as I am breathing your sorry soul will burn alongside me."

"Get out of my sight and be sure of this, you will pay for your stubbornness. Mark my words, you will be mine, Isadora."

Isadora walked out waving the stick in the air and feeling triumphant but she knew that once Peter reported her to the Rebecca, she would be in a lot of trouble.

The early morning chapel bells tolled but she ignored them, walking to the kitchen courtyard where more work awaited her. It was very early in the morning on Christmas Day. Her birthday and she was now twenty years old. Another dreadful day filled with painful memories.

26

WAVE OF SECRETS

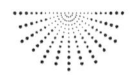

Rebecca cocked her arm back, hit Isadora with the whip hard. The girl gave only a single scream as she fell flat on the floor. Matron had a queer look on her face as if she was possessed of a demon and continued raining lashes on Isadora's back, tearing the light cotton blouse and the skin beneath it.

Isadora didn't scream again as she sometimes did, and neither did she beg Rebecca to stop. She didn't cry out. The only sounds in the room were the whip whooshing in the air and Rebecca's heavy laboured breathing.

If the newly appointed Sister Angelica hasn't been passing by, Isadora would have died from all the lashes she received that early morning. Sister

Angelica, a devoted servant of God, had started her own special labour in the workhouse at the request of Father John. He was concerned for the girl's safety and insisted that any further donations to the workhouse would only be considered if one of the sisters could live and work there to care for the souls of the ladies in the house. And care for them she did. She rushed into the room and grabbed Rebecca's hand before it made one more descent on the lacerated and bleeding back.

"Enough," she said in a firm voice, taking the whip. "Do you want to kill the girl?"

Her voice brought Rebecca back to her senses and she looked down at the unmoving girl.

"Are you proud of what you've done, Rebecca?"

"Don't talk to me like that," she replied as she pulled her hand away. "You don't know what this girl has done."

"It doesn't matter what she's done, no one deserves such a beating."

Rebecca merely sneered and walked out of the room. Angelica looked at the unconscious girl on the floor and shook her head. Trying as much as possible not to inflict any more harm on her, she half dragged and half carried Isadora to the bed where she placed her face down on it and then turned her head to the side so she wouldn't suffocate.

"I need to go and bring some balm and bandages to treat you," Angelica whispered to the still form. "But don't worry, I'll be back soon and will try to make sure that nothing like this ever happens to you again."

Because it was Christmas Day and there was much to be done, Angelica didn't return to the room until nearly an hour later and she was glad she got there just in time.

Slipping into unconsciousness, Isadora hadn't felt it when her body was carefully dragged to the bed and gently placed on it. She didn't feel the light sheet covering her or hear the gentle whispers of her rescuer, who left after some time. Neither did she see the figure that crept into her room nearly an hour later, nor feel him trying to pull her clothes aside. So bent was he on achieving what he had come for that he didn't notice the door opening.

"What do you think you're doing?" Sister Angelica entered the room and was just in time to stop the shady figure from stripping the wounded girl. "Who allowed you to come into this room?" Her eyes flashed at him and he turned to face her, his face burning.

"I came to tend to the girl."

"Does tending to her involve taking her clothes off?" And saying this, the incensed Angelica took a step further into the room. "I've heard a lot of complaints about you but ignored them because I thought the girls were just being silly and delusional. Now I know that what they said is true."

"Please," the pitiful man whimpered. "The devil came over me and I didn't know what to do."

"This young woman has been through enough torture and yet you wanted to add to her pain and shame. What kind of a man are you?"

"I won't repeat this again, please forgive me."

"Get out of this room before I scream for help!"

Peter scrambled out of the room.

Once he was gone, Sister Angelica cleaned Isadora's wounds and wept when she saw the damage done to the girl's back. These physical wounds would heal and maybe leave a scar or two, but the mental ones would take a long time to do so.

"Oh Child," she whispered, kneeling down beside the bed. "What did you ever do to deserve such pain and humiliation?" Still the figure made no response. Angelica was just glad that she had arrived in time to stop the wicked man. It seems Rebecca protected him because he was her nephew, the only son of her sister. Many girls had complained about him but they were punished for being evil.

"I'm going to keep a very close eye on you because there are so many enemies around here," she said. "It's so sad that you're an orphan and there's no one to take care of you." She shook her head. "It's Christmas Day and you should be with your friends heading to the dining hall for breakfast, yet here you are."

She rose to her feet and gently laid her hand on Isadora's shoulder.

"May the Lord have mercy on you and protect you," she whispered. "I'll try my best to protect you but the powers in this place are too strong for me alone." She raised her eyes heavenward. "Oh Lord, full of mercy and grace, watch over this poor child and protect her from all evil seen and unseen. If there's any way that you can get her out of here, please do so before her whole life and future is ruined by wicked people who are out to ruin her destiny." She quickly left the room, but not before locking it securely to ensure that no one could gain access to the girl inside.

As she walked away she continued to pray, "Lord, Grant us Your mercy and peace on this day as we celebrate the birth of Your only begotten Son," earnestly adding, "If only something would happen, if only."

27

THE MAIDEN'S TEARS

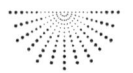

This was it, this was the end for her. "Help me," she whispered but knew that no one could hear her. At least the whipping had stopped. If Sister Angelica hadn't come in when she did, she would be dead. The pain was excruciating and she tried to cry but only dry heaves left her chest.

What had she ever done to Rebecca for the woman to hate her so much? The only respite she'd ever received was when she served as governess, far away from this place. Why had all who ever loved her abandoned her? As she slipped again into unconsciousness, she felt a gentle hand on her brow.

"Sleep child, God will soon bring you relief," she heard a soft voice telling her and she gave in to the darkness.

∾

Matron Rebecca always claimed that she was afraid of no one, but when she came face to face with Edgar Fontaine, her heart fainted within her. He looked like a man who could cause her a lot of trouble and she had to be careful how she handled him.

"I have it on good authority that my daughter Isadora is here, has been for the past eight years," the man said. "If you want any peace, you will show me at once where she is or call her to come here."

"Again, Mr. Fontaine, your daughter left for London three years ago to work as a governess. Perhaps she's somewhere in London."

Edgar laughed, a mirthless sound that shook Rebecca to the core. "Woman, do you take me for an imbecile? Your accomplice, Mrs. Clarissa Fontaine, who was my wife, died two days ago. Before she breathed her last, she confessed to all the wicked deeds she had done to my daughter, aided and abetted by yourself. The thing is this, not only did she tell me what she had done and how the two of you had planned to end my daughter's life, but the vicar, my son Arthur," he pointed at him. "and a bevy of servants were also present as witnesses. Many of us heard the awful accusations from my dying wife's lips that darkened your guilty name!" The words made Rebecca shake in her boots. "You didn't even leave her alone when she found work as a governess in London but had to bring her back here so you could continue tormenting her. What kind of a woman are you? Now, you are standing in my way. Just know this, if you don't bring me Isadora here dead or alive, you really have no idea what I will do to you."

"But sir," Rebecca was trembling inwardly.

"Did I ask you to speak?" Edgar roared.

"Papa," Arthur could see that his father had been pushed beyond the bonds of civility and he was about to explode. "Pa, please calm down. Isadora will be found," Arthur nodded to the servants who had accompanied them. "These men are prepared to tear this place to shreds to find my sister," he said. "You had better bring her out."

"I'm giving you only ten minutes to present her to me," Edgar's voice was cold and Rebecca shivered.

"Ten minutes, or you'll be sorry you ever heard the name Fontaine."

∼

Sister Angelica had seen the visitors and she crept into a side room to listen to the conversation. When she heard Isadora's name mentioned, her heart leapt for joy within her. Help had come for the girl, the Lord had answered her Christmas prayer and sent help just in time. But she knew that the Rebecca would seek to hide or harm the girl.

She quickly slipped back to the room where she had left Isadora and tried to rouse her but the child was still unconscious.

"What will I do?" She looked around the room as if she would find an answer there. She had to get Isadora out of here and to her family before Rebecca got the chance to do any more harm. Whatever happened, Isadora had to leave this workhouse today before something terrible befell her.

∼

"I'm here to see Rebecca," the important looking man stared down at the young lady who had opened the large door for him. "Would you please tell Miss Rebecca that chief constable Albert Ridge is here to see her?"

All the girls knew of constable Ridge, and the fact that he was standing here in St. Magdalene's meant something was going to happen. "And while you're at it, would you summon that man, Peter, too?"

"I don't know where Peter is at this moment," the frightened girl said.

"Then get me his aunt Rebecca."

"She has visitors."

"Show me to her office at once," the man looked fierce and the young girl nodded, leading the way. She was glad when she got to Rebecca's office and pointed out the door.

"This is Matron's office," and saying that, she fled. She would later tell her peers that the constable's eyes were so cold that she'd felt chilled right down to her bones.

∼

"If you don't send for my daughter at once, I'll cause such havoc in this place that in years to come, people will still be talking about it," Edgar was really frustrated. From the way the woman was hesitating, he was afraid that Isadora might have died and she didn't want to divulge that fact to him. "Where is Isadora?" There was a gentle but firm knock on the door and Rebecca looked somewhat relieved.

"I have to find out who that is," she hurried to the door but as soon as she opened it, Arthur saw her turn as white as a sheet and she stepped back.

When constable Ridge stepped into the room, Arthur looked at his father and then back at the man and his entourage. He seemed like a very important person and Rebecca was practically cowering at his feet, clearly shaken.

Albert looked around and his eyes lighted on Edgar. "Who are you?"

"My name is Edgar Fontaine and I'm here to take my daughter away from this hell."

"My dear good man, you sound really angry. Would you care to tell me about it?"

But Edgar was past the point of being civil. "I honour and respect you, sir, for you look like an important man. But if someone doesn't produce my daughter and let me take her back home, I'm going to cause such a ruckus that all of Oxford will hear of it."

Constable Albert chuckled, "No need to get so emotional and dramatic." He turned to one of the men with him. "Could you please find out where this man's daughter is and bring her here?"

"Her name is Isadora and if it isn't too much to ask, I'd like my son Arthur to go also."

Before they could leave, Sister Angelica boldly stepped into the room. All protocol had been broken but she didn't care. The life of a young woman hung in the balance. "Isadora is critically ill," Edgar didn't wait for her to finish speaking.

"I demand that you take me to her at once," he said.

"And I'm happy to do so."

Constable Ridge didn't know whether to laugh or scold everyone in sight. No one seemed to care who he was or what his mission to St. Magdalene's was. He could see from the face of the irate father that if anyone stood in his way, they would probably be trampled underfoot so he just shook his head and stepped aside, giving Rebecca a very cold look.

"This clearly shows me that there are a lot of issues to be addressed in this place," was all he said before taking a seat.

∽

Arthur wept when he saw Isadora. Someone had bandaged her back but he saw the torn and bloodied blouse in the corner.

"Hold yourself, son," Edgar said in a shaky voice. "We've found her and we are getting her out of this place right now."

"Oh Father."

Edgar was glad he'd brought the large carriage and a soft bed was made on the floor of it for Isadora. The other girls did all they could to help and he was glad that Rebecca stayed out of his way. But he had some final words to say to her once Isadora had been carried out to the carriage and Arthur was watching over her. They would never let her out of their sight again.

"If my daughter dies as a result of the beating you gave her, just know this. I will do everything in my power including using all the influence I have with people in authority, to make sure that you're locked up in jail for the rest of your miserable life."

28
SILKEN TRUTH

She was either dead or dreaming, the kind of dream that a person never wants to wake up from. She could hear soft murmuring but the voices kept fading away then becoming loud again. What she didn't know was that she kept drifting in and out of consciousness.

Where was this, she wondered, where am I? The bed felt very soft and all the pain was gone. She was lying on her stomach and felt as if she was floating in the air.

"Her spirit is broken," a strange voice finally broke through the fog in her mind. "It's as though the girl has given up all her will to live." Who were these people and who were they talking about?

"What can we do, Doctor?"

Wait, that was her father's voice. But he was dead, and had been for these past eight years. This could only mean one thing, that she too had finally given up the ghost.

"You have to call her back from the brink of despair. I've seen patients in this state and they never came back. Facing life on this side was so terrible that they preferred to die. If she feels your love, she will come back. But I ask that you don't leave her alone, not for a single moment. Read to her, talk to her and jog her out of this condition that she has sunk into."

∼

Isadora couldn't believe that it was still Christmas Day. The hours seemed to be dragging and she was tired of it all. But she was alive and had finally recognized where she was; at home and in her own bed after eight long years.

She expected her stepmother to burst into the room at any moment and order her out of bed, telling her that she was pretending.

None of that happened, however, and instead it was Arthur and her father who came in. They both looked a little fearful and she closed her eyes to shut them out.

"Isadora," her father came over to the bed. "Please open your eyes and look at me."

"Why?" She whispered keeping her eyes tight shut.

"Isadora, we don't know how you will ever forgive us for what happened to you."

"It isn't important," she turned her head to face the wall. "I'm not important."

"Don't say that, Isadora," Arthur joined his father in pleading with her. "You're very important to us."

"Then why did you allow Clarissa to send me to that horrible place and keep me there? They wanted to kill me and you should just have left me there to die so that I would no longer be a bother to you."

"Isadora," her father gasped.

"I'm tired," she said. "I want to sleep."

Isadora slipped into a painful, storm tossed and dreamless sleep.

29
VALLEY OF DECISION

She was exhausted but she'd made it to the vicar's house. It was just some minutes after noonday but it felt like so many hours had passed. She still couldn't believe that only days before she had woken up in the workhouse, confronted the lecherous Peter, received the beating of her life and was now here at home. She didn't realise she had been unconscious and days had passed while her body began to mend. Despite her pain she needed answers, and rose from her bed, carefully dressed and left the house.

"Come in," Reverend George Simms, the Vicar opened the door immediately after she knocked. They must have seen her coming up the path. "Isadora, I can't believe that it's you," he said. "Please do come in."

"Thank you," Isadora was glad to be out of the cold. As she entered the small living room, she saw Salome Simms, the vicar's wife placing a tray on the table. She had interrupted their midday meal but she had nowhere else to go.

The house was warm and smelled of cinnamon buns and cookies just like it had years ago and she closed her eyes to take in the aroma.

Salome walked over to her, observed her for a moment and then held out her arms. Isadora didn't hesitate but walked into them like she had always done. The embrace was so warm, full of love, acceptance and understanding and Isadora immediately burst into tears. No one had ever held her so close or so lovingly and she held on and wouldn't let go. She didn't even mind the pain on her back when Mrs. Salome put her arms around her and squeezed.

It took her a while to calm down but she finally did. "I'm sorry," she gave a shaky laugh. "I don't know what came over me."

"Child, you don't need to apologise for being human," Salome held her hand and then led her to the couch. "Isadora, you've been through so much in the past eight years that you deserve a rest and a break. Carrying a heavy burden for so long like you have can be quite daunting so you're allowed to shed tears to find relief."

"Thank you."

~

"Pa!" Arthur's panicked voice made Edgar shoot to his feet. "Pa, Isadora is gone."

"What do you mean she's gone?"

"I sent Rose up to her bedroom to check and see if she needed anything but she found the bed and room empty."

"Are you sure she hasn't gone to the outhouse?'

"We've checked and searched everywhere, but she's gone," Arthur was so pale that his father thought he would faint. "Pa, I can't lose her again."

"And you won't," Edgar promised. He had failed these children before, he wasn't going to do it again. "Call all the servants and tell them that I wish to speak to them."

"Yes, Pa."

"I'm so sad," Isadora said, wiping her eyes. "I suffered for six years because my stepmother hated me so much. The only time I got any respite was the two years that I went to London to work for Mr. and Mrs. Wallace. But in the end, even that didn't matter," she twisted her lips. "There's a curse upon my life because I'm an abomination to the whole world," she covered her face with the palms of her hands. "They should have just left me there to die."

"Don't say that," Salome put a gentle arm on her shoulder.

"I committed a sin that can never be forgiven so why should I take any pleasure in life? My end is hell and eternal damnation."

Isadora was surprised to hear the Vicar chuckling softly. "Dear child, someone has really played with your mind. What do you consider as the unpardonable sin?" He asked her.

Isadora twisted her fingers in her lap. "When I was twelve on Christmas Day eight years ago, Arthur and I were reading and then we fell asleep on his bed," her face flamed at the shame.

"Go on," Salome encouraged in a soft voice.

"My stepmother found us and told Papa that she had caught me laying in carnality with my brother. Papa was so angry that he left and didn't come back. Five days later, we received news that his ship had sunk. My stepmother said I was an evil child who had brought a curse on the family and caused my father's death. I deserved to be punished because I committed the unpardonable sin."

The vicar came and sat on the seat opposite hers. "Isadora, you need to understand one thing. Eight years ago, Arthur came here the day after you were taken away. His mother had told him that you ran away in the night and he was so miserable because he hadn't defended you. He believed it was the reason you ran away from home."

"I never ran away from home," Isadora said passionately. "My stepmother had them come and take me away."

"That's what she wanted everyone to believe, that you ran away. But that's all in the past now. You've got to remember that at the time Arthur was also still a child himself and didn't know what to do. For five years, he tried to find you on his own but didn't know what to do. We both tried," he shrugged. "When your father came back three years ago, they went on with the search."

That was news to Isadora. "Pa came back only three years ago? Where was he?"

The vicar quickly filled her in on what he knew, "But they have to tell you the whole story themselves and I pray that you will listen."

Isadora shook her head, "I can't continue living in that house with them."

"Why not? They came looking for you, doesn't that tell you something?" She merely shrugged. "Isadora," the Vicar's voice was loving but firm. "They want you, need you because they love you so much. You've got to give them the chance to prove that to you."

"I just can't stay in that house."

"Give me a good reason for that."

Isadora turned a bright red and the vicar and his wife looked at each other then nodded in understanding.

"Is it because of Arthur?" Salome asked "And how you feel about him?"

Isadora gave them a startled look. She expected to find condemnation or disgust in their eyes but all she saw was understanding. "How did you know?"

"You have a very expressive face and he also came here not too long ago to confess the same thing."

"He did?"

Reverend Simms nodded, "The poor boy was so torn up about it. But all is well now, Isadora, the two of you aren't related in any way."

"What?"

"It's true but like I said, it's for your father and brother to tell you the truth themselves. Now, why don't we take you back home so you can be properly reconciled to your family?"

∾

THANK YOU FOR CHOOSING A PUREREAD BOOK!

We hope you enjoyed the story, and as a way to thank you for choosing PureRead we'd like to send you this free book, and other fun reader rewards…

Click here for your free copy of Whitechapel Waif
PureRead.com/victorian

Thanks again for reading.
See you soon!

OUR GIFT TO YOU

AS A WAY TO SAY THANK YOU WE WOULD LOVE TO SEND YOU THIS BEAUTIFUL STORY FREE OF CHARGE.

Our Reader List is 100% FREE

Click here for your free copy of Whitechapel Waif

PureRead.com/victorian

At PureRead we publish books you can trust. Great tales without smut or swearing, but with all of the mystery and romance you expect from a great story.

Be the first to know when we release new books, take part in our fun competitions, and get surprise free books in your inbox by signing up to our Reader list.

As a thank you you'll receive an exclusive copy of Whitechapel Waif - a beautiful book available only to our subscribers...

Click here for your free copy of Whitechapel Waif

PureRead.com/victorian

Printed in Great Britain
by Amazon